OKAY, I've *seen* them before. Naked guys, I mean. On TV. In New York, when I go there for UN stuff, there's a whole public access channel devoted to naked guys.

And of course I've seen pictures of Michelangelo's statue of David. Not to mention all the rest of the classical art at the National Gallery, which is, you know. Mostly nudes.

But the first naked guy that I ever saw *live* and *up close*? I totally didn't expect it to be someone I hadn't even known five minutes before.

To tell you the truth, I thought the first naked guy I'd ever see up close and personal like that would be my boyfriend, David.

Or so I'd been *hoping*. Boy, had *that* not worked out according to plan.

THE PRINCESS DIARIES, VOLUME VII:
PARTY PRINCESS

SWEET SIXTEEN PRINCESS:
A PRINCESS DIARIES BOOK (VOLUME VII AND A HALF)

THE PRINCESS DIARIES, VOLUME VIII:
PRINCESS ON THE BRINK

THE PRINCESS DIARIES, VOLUME IX:
PRINCESS MIA

ILLUSTRATED BY CHESLEY MCLAREN:

PRINCESS LESSONS: A PRINCESS DIARIES BOOK

PERFECT PRINCESS: A PRINCESS DIARIES BOOK

HOLIDAY PRINCESS: A PRINCESS DIARIES BOOK

THE MEDIATOR BOOKS:

THE MEDIATOR 1: SHADOWLAND

THE MEDIATOR 2: NINTH KEY

THE MEDIATOR 3: REUNION

THE MEDIATOR 4: DARKEST HOUR

THE MEDIATOR 5: HAUNTED

THE MEDIATOR 6: TWILIGHT

THE 1-800-WHERE-R-YOU BOOKS:

1: WHEN LIGHTNING STRIKES

2: CODE NAME CASSANDRA

3: SAFE HOUSE

4: SANCTUARY

5: MISSING YOU

MEG CABOT

READY OR NOT

* AN ALL-AMERICAN GIRL NOVEL *

HARPER TEEN
AN IMPRINT OF HARPERCOLLINS PUBLISHERS

HarperTeen is an imprint
of HarperCollins Publishers.

Library of Congress Cataloging-in-Publication Data
Cabot, Meg.
   Ready or not: an all-American girl novel / Meg
Cabot.—1st ed.
      p.   cm.
   Summary: Now a high school junior, Samantha
tries to decide whether she is ready to have sex with
her boyfriend, who happens to be the President's son.
   ISBN 978-0-06-147996-0
   [1. Sex—Fiction. 2. Presidents—Fiction. 3. High
schools—Fiction. 4. Schools—Fiction. 5. Family
life—Washington (D.C.)—Fiction. 6. Washington
(D.C.)—Fiction. 7. Humorous stories.] I. Title.
PZ7.C11165Re 2005   2004030044
[Fic]—dc22

❖

Revised HarperTeen paperback edition, 2008

TO LAURA LANGLIE,

a great agent and an even better friend

ACKNOWLEDGMENTS

Many thanks to Beth Ader, Jennifer Brown,
Michele Jaffe, Laura Langlie, Abigail McAden,
and, most of all, Benjamin Egnatz.

"*NEVER* doubt that a small group of committed people can change the world; indeed, it is the only thing that ever has."

—*Margaret Mead, anthropologist*

"*AFTER* you make a fool of yourself a few hundred times, you learn what works."

—*Gwen Stefani*

$Okay$, here are the top ten reasons it sucks to be me, Samantha Madison:

10. In spite of the fact that last year I saved the life of the president of the United States, got a medal for heroism, and had a movie made about me, I continue to be one of the least popular people in my entire school, which is supposed to be a progressive and highly rated institution, but which seems to me to be entirely populated, with the exception of myself and my best friend Catherine, by Abercrombie-and-Fitch-wearing, zero-tolerance-for-anyone-who-might-actually-have-a-different-opinion-than-their-own (or, actually, *any* opinion at all), blithely-school-song-chanting, reality-TV-show-watching neo-fascists.

9. My older sister—the one who apparently got all the good DNA, like the genes for strawberry-blond, silky-smooth hair, as opposed to copper-red, Brillo pad–textured hair—is the most popular girl at Adams Prep (and can, in fact, often be found leading the blithe school song chanters there), causing me to be asked on an almost daily basis by students, teachers, and even my own parents, as they observe me being tossed about the social strata, a lone depressive in a sea of endless pep: "Why can't you be more like your sister Lucy?"

8. Even though I was appointed teen ambassador to the United Nations due to my alleged bravery in saving the president, I rarely get out of school to perform my duties. Nor, incidentally, am I paid for them.

7. Because of this, I have been forced to get an actual wage-earning job in addition to my apparently strictly volunteer work as teen ambassador to pay my ever-mounting bill at Sullivan's Art Supplies, where I have to buy my own Strathmore drawing pads and lead pencils, since my parents have decided I need to learn

the value of a dollar and acquire a "work ethic."

And unlike my sister Lucy, who was also required to get a job in order to keep her in paint—the facial, not the art variety—I did not find employment in a cushy lingerie store at the mall that gives me a thirty percent discount and pays me ten bucks an hour to sit behind a desk and read magazines until a customer deigns to ask me a question about crotchless panties.

No, instead I got a crappy practically-minimum-wage-paying job at Potomac Video rewinding horrible Brittany Murphy movies and then putting them back on the shelves for more people to rent and be sucked into Brittany Murphy's sick, twisted, Look-At-How-Much-Weight-I've-Lost-Since-I-Did-*Clueless*-and-Ashton-Broke-Up-with-Me-for-Dried-Up-Demi-and-I-Became-a-Bigger-Star-Than-Him, psycho, scrunchy-faced world.

And okay, at least I get to hang out with cool high school dropouts, like my new multipierced friend, Dauntra.

But still.

6. Between school, art lessons, my duties as teen ambassador, and my job, I have only one night

a week to see my boyfriend in anything
remotely resembling a social context.

5. As my boyfriend is as busy as I am, plus is also
filling out college applications for next year, *and*
happens to be the president's son (and is
therefore frequently called upon to attend state
functions the one night I can do stuff with him), I
either have to do the boring state function stuff
with him, which doesn't leave a whole lot of
time for romance, or sit at home watching
National Geographic Explorer with my twelve-
year-old sister, Rebecca, every Saturday night.

4. I am the only nearly-seventeen-year-old girl on
the planet who has seen every episode of
National Geographic Explorer. And despite the
fact that my mother is an environmental lawyer,
I don't actually care that much about the melting
polar ice caps. I'd much rather make out with
my boyfriend.

3. Regardless of the fact that I once saved the life of
the president of the United States, I still have not
met my idol, Gwen Stefani (although she did
send me a jean jacket from her clothing line,
L.A.M.B., when she heard I consider myself her

number-one fan. However, the first day I wore said jacket to Adams Prep, I received many scathing remarks from my fellow students about it, such as, "Punk much?" and "Which way to the mosh pit?" revealing that fashion forwardness is still not a valued character trait in my peer group).

2. Everyone who is the least bit acquainted with me *knows* all this, and yet *still* persists in gushing to me about how fab my life is, and how I ought to be grateful for all the great things I have, like that boyfriend I never get to see and those parents who send me to such a great school where everyone hates my guts. Oh, and my close personal relationship with the president, who sometimes can't remember my name, in spite of the fact that I broke my arm in two places saving his life.

And the number-one reason it sucks to be me, Samantha Madison:

1. Unless something drastically changes, it doesn't look like things are going to get better anytime soon.

1

Which might explain why I finally got the guts to do it.

Make a change, I mean. And a pretty big one, too. For the better.

Who cares if my sister Lucy doesn't necessarily agree?

Actually, she didn't say she didn't like it. Not that I would have cared if she had. I didn't do it for her. I did it for myself.

Which is how I replied to her. Lucy, I mean. When she said what she did about it, which was: "Mom's going to kill you."

"I didn't do it for Mom," I said. "I did it for me. No one else."

I don't even know what she was doing home. Lucy, I mean. Shouldn't she have been at cheerleading practice? Or a game? Or shopping at the

6

mall with her friends, which is how she spends the vast majority of her time, when she isn't *working* at the mall—which amounts to almost the same thing, since all her friends hang out in Bare Essentials (the lingerie store where she gets paid to do nothing), while she's there anyway, helping her squeal over the latest J.Lo gossip in *Us Weekly* and fold G-strings?

"Yeah, but you don't have to look at yourself," Lucy said from her desk. I could tell she was IMing her boyfriend, Jack. Lucy has to IM him every morning before school, and then again before bed, and sometimes, like now, even in between, or he gets upset. Jack is away at college at the Rhode Island School of Design and has proved, since he left, to be increasingly insecure about Lucy's affections for him. He needs near-constant reassurances that she still cares about him and isn't off making out with some dude she met at Sunglass Hut, or whatever.

Which is kind of surprising, because before he left for college, Jack never struck me as the needy type. I guess college can change people.

This isn't a very encouraging thought, considering that *my* boyfriend, who is Lucy's age, will be going off to college next year. At least

Jack drives down to see Lucy every weekend, which is nice, instead of hanging with his college friends. I hope David will do this as well.

Although I'm beginning to wonder if Jack actually even has any. College friends, I mean.

"I have to look at myself in the mirror all the time," is what I said to Lucy's remark about how I don't have to look at myself. "Besides, no one asked you."

And I turned to continue down the hallway, which is where I'd been headed when Lucy had stopped me, having spied me attempting to slink past her open bedroom door.

"Fine," Lucy called after me, as I attempted to slink away again. "But just so you know, you don't look like her."

Of course I had to come back to her doorway and go, "Like who?" Because I genuinely had no idea what she was talking about. Although you would think by this time, I would have known better than to ask. I mean, it was *Lucy* I was talking to.

"You know," she said, after taking a sip of her diet Coke. "Your hero. What's her name. Gwen Stefani. She has blond hair, right? Not black."

Oh my God. I couldn't believe Lucy was

trying to tell me—*me*, Gwen Stefani's number-one fan—what color hair she has.

"I am aware of that," I said, and started to leave again.

But Lucy's next remark brought me right back to her doorway.

"Now you look like that other chick. What's her name?"

"Karen O?" I asked, hopefully. Don't even *ask* me why I thought Lucy might be about to say something nice, like that I looked like the lead singer of the Yeah Yeah Yeahs. I think I had inhaled too much ammonium hydroxide from the hair dye, or something.

"Nuh-uh," Lucy said. Then she snapped her fingers. "Got it. Ashlee Simpson."

I sucked in my breath. There are way worse things than looking like Ashlee Simpson—who actually looks fine—but it's the idea that people might think I was trying to *copy* her that so utterly repulsed me that I could feel the Doritos I'd scarfed after school rising in my throat. I couldn't actually think of anything worse at that particular moment. In fact, at that particular moment, it was lucky for Lucy there was nothing sharp sitting around nearby, or I swear, I think I might have stabbed her.

"I do *not* look like Ashlee Simpson," I managed to croak.

Lucy just shrugged and turned back to her computer screen, as usual showing no remorse whatsoever for her actions.

"Whatever," she said. "I'm sure David's dad is going to be thrilled. Don't you have to go on VH1 or something next week to promote his stupid Return to Family thingie?"

"MTV," I said, feeling even worse, because now I was remembering that I still hadn't read any of the stuff Mr. Green, the White House press secretary, had given to me in preparation for that particular event. I mean, come on. Between homework and drawing lessons and work, how much time do I even have for teen ambassador stuff? That would be zero.

Besides, a girl has to have her priorities. And mine was dyeing my hair.

So that I looked like an Ashlee Simpson wannabe, apparently.

"And you know perfectly well it's MTV," I snapped at Lucy, because I was still smarting over the Ashlee thing. Also because I was mad at myself for not having started studying up on the

10

stuff I was supposed to say. But better to take it out on Lucy than myself. "And that it's a town hall meeting, and the president will be there. At Adams Prep. Like you weren't planning on going to it and using the opportunity to test out those new pink jeans you got from Betsey Johnson."

Lucy looked all innocent. "I don't know what you're talking about."

"You are so full of it!" I couldn't believe she had the nerve to sit there and pretend like that. Like anyone at school could talk about anything else. That MTV was coming to Adams Prep, I mean. No one could care less that the *president* was coming. It was the hot new VJ, Random Alvarez (Seriously. That's his name. Random), who was hosting the stupid thing, that Lucy and her friends were all excited about.

Not just Lucy and her friends, either. Kris Parks (who happens to have a particular personal dislike for me, though she tries to hide it, seeing as how I'm a national heroine and all. But I can tell it's still there, just brewing under the surface of her *Hi, Sam, how are you*'s), panicked recently that her transcript isn't crammed with enough extracurriculars (considering she's *only* a varsity cheerleader, a National Merit Scholar,

11

and president of our class), founded this new club, Right Way, that is supposed to be this big call to action for teens to take back their right to say no to drugs, alcohol, and sex.

Although to tell you the truth, I didn't actually know this right had ever been threatened. I mean, as far as I knew, no one has actually ever gotten *mad* at people who say no thanks to a beer or whatever. Except maybe a girl's boyfriend, when she wouldn't, you know, Do It with him.

I had, however, noticed that whenever word got around that a girl had, you know, Gone All the Way with her boyfriend, Kris Parks in particular, and her fellow Right Way-ers in general, were always the first to call that girl a slut, generally to her face.

Anyway, because of Right Way, Kris is one of the people who is going to be on the student panel during the president's town hall meeting at Adams Prep. All she'd been able to talk about since finding this out was how this is her big chance to impress all the Ivy League universities who are going to be beating down her door, begging her to attend them. Also how she is going to get to meet Random Alvarez, and how she is going to give him her cell number, and how they are going to start dating.

Like Random would look at Kris twice, since I heard he's dating Paris Hilton. Although "dating" might be the wrong word for it. But whatever.

"Anyway," I said to Lucy, "for your information, that happens to be *why* I did it. Dyed my hair, I mean. I need a new look for the town meeting. Something less . . . girl-who-saved-the-president. You know?"

"Well, you certainly accomplished that," was all Lucy said. Then she added, "And Mom's still going to kill you," before she went back to IMing Jack, since he'd sent her two messages that she'd ignored during the time I'd walked back into the room. You could bet he wasn't too happy about her not paying attention to him. Like he thought maybe she was paying attention to her *other* boyfriend (the imaginary one, from Sunglass Hut) instead of him for a minute.

At least, that's how it sounded from the angry pinging.

I told myself I don't care what Lucy thinks. What does she know about fashion, anyway? Oh, sure, she reads *Vogue* every month from front to back.

13

But I'm not going for the kind of look you could find in *Vogue*. Unlike Lucy, I am not a fashion conformist. I am striving for my own personal sense of style, not one dictated to me by any magazine.

Or Ashlee Simpson.

Still, when I went downstairs to get my jacket before heading downtown, I have to say, I'd expected a better reaction to my new look than the one I received from Theresa, our housekeeper.

"Santa María, what have you done to your head?" she wanted to know.

I put a hand up to my hair, sort of defensively. "You don't like it?"

Theresa just shook her head and called once more upon Jesus' mom. Though I don't know what *she* was supposed to do about it.

My younger sister, Rebecca, looked up from her homework—she goes to a different school than Lucy and I do. In fact, Rebecca goes to a school for gifted kids, Horizon, the same school my boyfriend, David, goes to, where they don't have cheerleaders *or* pep rallies or even grades and everyone has to wear a uniform so no one makes fun of other people's fashion sense. I wish

I could go there instead of Adams Prep. Only you practically have to be a genius to go to Horizon. And while I am what my guidance counselor, Mrs. Flynn, likes to call "above average," I'm no genius.

"I think you look good," was Rebecca's verdict on my hair.

"Really?" I wanted to kiss her.

Until she added, "Yeah. Like Joan of Arc. Not that anyone really knows what Joan of Arc looked like, since there is only one known portrait of her, and that was one doodled into the margin of the court record of the trial where she was condemned to death for witchcraft. But you look sort of like it. The doodle, I mean."

While this was better than being told I looked like Ashlee Simpson, it's not very comforting to be told you look like a doodle, either. Even a doodle of Joan of Arc.

"Your parents are going to kill me," Theresa said.

This was worse than being told I looked like a doodle.

"They'll get over it," I said. Sort of more hopefully than I felt.

"Is it permanent?" Theresa wanted to know.

"Semi," I said.

"Santa María," Theresa said, again. Then, noticing I had my jacket on, she was all, "Where do you think you're going?"

"Art lessons," I said.

"I thought you had those on Mondays and Wednesdays this year. Today's Thursday." You can't pull anything over on Theresa. Believe me. I've tried.

"I do," I said. "Normally. This is a new class. For adults only." Susan Boone owns the art studio where my boyfriend and I take drawing lessons. Sometimes it's the only time I get to see him since we're both so busy, and go to different schools, and all.

Not that this is why I go to them. Drawing lessons, I mean. I go to learn to become a master at my craft, not to make out with my boyfriend.

Although we do usually get in a few kisses in the stairwell after class.

"Susan said she thought David and I were ready," I said.

"Ready for what?" Theresa wanted to know.

"A more advanced class," I said. "A special one."

"What kind of special class?"

"Life drawing," I explained. I'm used to getting the third degree from Theresa. She's been working for our family for a million years and is sort of like our second mom. Well, really, she's more like our *first* mom, since we hardly ever see our real mom, on account of her busy environmental law career. Theresa has a bunch of other kids, all of whom are grown, and even some grandkids, so she's pretty much seen it all.

Except life drawing, apparently, since she went, all suspiciously, "What's that?"

"You know," I said, more confidently than I felt, since I wasn't entirely sure what it was myself. "As opposed to still lifes, piles of fruit and stuff. Instead of objects, we'll be drawing living things . . . people."

I have to admit, I was kind of excited at the prospect of finally getting to draw something— *anything*—other than cow horns or grapes. Probably only geeks get excited about this kind of thing but, hey, whatever. So I'm a geek. With my new hair, at least I'm a goth geek.

Susan had made a big deal out of it, too. The fact that she was letting David and me come to a life drawing class, I mean. We would, she said, be the youngest people there, seeing as how it was an adult class. "But I think you're both mature enough to handle it," is what Susan had said.

Being almost seventeen, and all, I should certainly *hope* I was mature enough to handle it. I mean, what did she think I was going to do, anyway? Throw spitwads at the model?

"I didn't know I'd have to drive you downtown." Theresa looked annoyed. "I have to take Rebecca to her karate lesson——"

"Qigong," Rebecca corrected her.

"Whatever," Theresa said. "The art studio's all the way downtown, the opposite direction——"

"Relax," I said. "I'm taking the Metro."

Theresa looked shocked. "But you can't. You remember what happened last time."

Yeah. Nice of her to remind me. Last time I'd tried to ride the Metro, I'd run smack into a family reunion——literally all of these people wearing these bright yellow T-shirts that said *Caution: Johnson Family Vacation In Progress*, who'd recognized me, then swarmed all over me, asking if I was the girl who'd saved the president, and demanding that I sign each of their T-shirts. They'd caused such a commotion——the Johnson family was pretty extended——that the transit police had had to come over and peel them off me. Then they'd politely asked me not to ride the rails anymore.

The transit police, I mean. Not the Johnson family.

"Yeah," I said. "Well, last time my hair was still red, and people could recognize me. Now"—I patted my new hair—"they won't."

Theresa continued to look worried.

"But your parents—"

"—want me to learn a work ethic," I said. "What better way than for me to take public transportation, like the rest of the plebeians?"

I could tell Rebecca was impressed by my use of the word "plebeian," which I'd gotten from Lucy's SAT prep book. Not that Lucy had spent any time actually studying it. At least if her reaction the time I called her a succubus (SAT word meaning "a demon or fiend; especially, a lascivious spirit supposed to have sexual intercourse with men by night without their knowledge") was any indication, seeing as how she took it as a compliment.

It wasn't easy, beating Theresa off, but I finally managed it. When are people going to realize that I'm nearly an adult, old enough to fend for myself? I mean, apparently I'm mature enough for life drawing classes—not to mention a part-time job—but not old enough to ride the Metro by myself?

Whatever. In any other state, I'd have my own car by now. Just my luck to live in an area where the rules to get a driver's license are almost as restrictive as the ones to get a gun license.

In the end, Theresa let me go . . . but only because what choice did she have, really? With Dad working later than ever at his office at the World Bank, and Mom all tied up in her latest case, it wasn't like Theresa could really call them for backup. They barely got home in time for dinner anymore—they'd given up on the whole concept of us ever finding time to sit down together as a family and eat—let alone to super-vise us.

Not that we need supervision. We're all pretty much caught up in our own routines: art lessons, Potomac Video, or teen ambassador stuff for me every day after school; cheerleading or the mall—either to work or socialize—for Lucy; and Rebecca . . . well, between clarinet lessons, chess club meetings, qigong, and what-ever else goes on in her bizarre, girl-genius world, it's a wonder any of us ever even see her.

I was glad to get out of the house and into the crisp November air. I was also glad that my duties as teen ambassador had forced the White House to get me my own cell phone. This is the kind of thing I'm supposed to be learning to save up for with the money from my part-time job. Lucy has to pay for her own phone (well, for any calls that aren't to Mom or Dad, anyway, asking if she can stay later at whichever party she's currently attending).

I, on the other hand, get my phone free.

Being a national hero does have its perks, I guess.

"Hello?" I was relieved my best friend, Catherine, and not her parents or younger brothers, had answered. Catherine doesn't have a cell phone, so I'd had to call her on her family's land line.

"It's me," I said. "I did it."

"How's it look?" Catherine asked.

"I think it looks okay," I said. "Rebecca says I look like Joan of Arc."

"She was cute," Catherine said, encouragingly "Until she burned up, anyway. What did Lucy say?"

"That I look like Ashlee Simpson."

"Super cute!" Catherine cooed.

See, this is the problem with Catherine. I mean, she's my best friend, and I love her to death. But sometimes she says things like this, and I fear for her. I really do. Because what's going to happen to her when she gets out into the real world? She's just going to get eaten alive.

"Catherine," I said. "I don't want people to think I'm copying Ashlee Simpson's look. That would not be cool."

"Oh," Catherine said. "Okay. Sorry." She appeared to think about this for a minute. Then she asked, "Well . . . what else did Lucy say?"

"That Mom's going to kill me."

"Oh," Catherine said. "That's not good."

"I don't care," I said, as I hurried down the leaf-strewn street.

We live in Cleveland Park, a section of Washington, D.C., that isn't actually that far from 1600 Pennsylvania Avenue, a.k.a. the White House, where my boyfriend lives. Most everyone who goes to Adams Prep lives in my neighborhood or Chevy Chase, the next neighborhood over, where Lucy's boyfriend, Jack, lived before he went to college.

"It's my head," I said into the phone. "I should

be able to do what I want to it."

"Power to the people," Catherine agreed. "Are you going to the studio now?"

"Yes," I said. "I'm Metro-ing it."

"Good luck," Catherine said. "Look out for any Johnson Family Vacations In Progress. And let me know what David says. About your hair."

"Over and out," I said into the phone, as a sort of joke, because this was how we'd signed off on our walkie-talkies as kids. Really, cell phones are just like walkie-talkies. They just cost more. The sad thing is, Catherine's parents won't get her one, so it's kind of a one-sided experience. Catherine's parents are very strict and won't even let her talk on the phone to boys, let alone date, except group dates, which made it quite hard on her and her boyfriend . . . back when she still had one. Sadly for Catherine, her boyfriend's diplomat father got himself transferred to Qatar, and now she and Paul are doing the long-distance thing, like Lucy and Jack. . . .

Only Qatar is a lot farther away than Rhode Island, so Paul can never drive down for the weekend.

Catherine's parents, in addition to not getting her a cell phone, would *never* let her ride the

Metro alone. Actually, mine wouldn't have been too thrilled about it, either, if they'd known. Not because of them being afraid I might get lost or abducted and sold into white slavery (which happens a lot more in the Midwest, at places like the Mall of America, than it does on the Metro . . . I know because Rebecca and I watched an episode of *National Geographic Explorer* about it) but because of the whole Johnson Family Vacation In Progress thing.

Sadly, it doesn't worry them enough to get me out of my job at Potomac Video.

But I could see right away that, thanks to my new hair color, things were going to be different. No one on the train recognized me. No one even glanced at me twice, as if trying to remember where they'd seen me before. I made it all the way to R Street and Connecticut—right across from the Founding Church of Scientology— where Susan Boone's art studio is located, without out a single person going, "Hey, aren't you Samantha Madison?" or "Hey, wasn't there a movie made about you last summer?"

I was so excited about not being recognized for once that I ran right past Static, the record shop next door to the studio, without even stopping to see if they'd got anything good in . . . though I did pause to admire my reflection in the store window. I was stoked that I apparently looked so different that people didn't even know who I was.

Because, as far as I'm concerned, different can only mean better.

Although I wasn't quite sure that David, when he got to the studio a few minutes after I did, agreed. He glanced my way, then went right past me, as if he were looking for someone else . . .

. . . then did a double-take when he realized the girl straddling the drawing bench in front of him was really me.

I couldn't tell from his expression if he liked my hair or not. I mean, he was smiling, but that didn't mean anything. David is generally a happy guy—not at all moody, like Jack, Lucy's boyfriend, even though in his own way, David is every bit as talented an artist as Jack, if not more so. Even if that's just my opinion.

It's also my opinion that David's a lot better looking than Jack, with his green eyes—no, really. They're *green*. Not hazel, either, but pure green, like the grass on the Great Lawn in springtime—and kind of floppy, dark, curly hair.

Not that it's a competition—whose boyfriend

is hotter, mine or my sister's.

But the truth is, mine totally is. Even though we've been going out for more than a year, my heart still does this funny, zingy thing every time I see him . . . David, I mean. Rebecca says this is called frisson.

I don't care what it's called, or what causes it. All I know is, I love David. He's just so . . . *there*. When he walks into a room, he doesn't just walk into it . . . he *fills* it, I guess on account of being so tall and big-boned and everything. When he kisses me, he has to stoop way down to reach my lips, and a lot of the time, he cups my face in his hands to hold it steady. . . .

It's super hot.

But not as hot as the way he looks at me sometimes . . . like now, for instance.

My parents, in addition to their "work ethic" thing, have also been on this autonomy kick (meaning that we have to start doing our own laundry now, instead of Theresa doing it) so that we learn how to function as normal—i.e., clean—members of society. So the only clean thing I'd been able to find to wear to class, since I hadn't remembered to do my laundry, was this black shirt Nike had sent me, in the hopes I'd wear it the next time I went on TV—like at the town hall meeting on MTV next week.

Which is definitely another perk of being a national heroine . . . getting free clothes, and all.

Only, fond as I am of Nike, I try not to engage in blatant product placement. So I had never put on this shirt before. Which was why I didn't know until I saw David's face that it must be kind of sexy. The shirt, I mean. I don't have big boobs—or little ones, really. Just normal-sized—but I guess this shirt must be sort of tight and I guess it makes what boobage I do have stick out more than usual . . . plus it has a V-neck, so it definitely shows more cleavage than the shirts I usually wear.

Which might explain why, when David finally recognized me, he didn't even *notice* my hair. The minute he spotted me, his gaze went straight to my chest. Then, when he went to sit down on the drawing bench next to mine, all he said was, "Hey, Sharona."

"Hey, Daryl," I said back to him.

Daryl and Sharona are our white trash names. You know, what we think our names would be if we'd been born in a trailer park instead of Cleveland Park (me) or Houston, Texas (David).

Which is not to say that anyone who has the name Daryl or Sharona is necessarily white trash, or that anyone who lives in a trailer park is, either. Just that if *we* were white trash, they'd be the names we thought we'd have. . . .

Okay, it's a couple thing. You know how people who've been going out a long time have these couple things that they do? Like my mom and dad call each other "Schmoopie" sometimes, after an episode of a sitcom they saw once. The Daryl and Sharona thing is like that.

Only not repulsive.

"I like your shirt," was what Daryl/David said next.

"Yeah," I said. "That part was sort of obvious."

"You should wear shirts like that more often," Daryl/David said, not even looking the least bit ashamed of himself for so blatantly ogling (SAT word meaning "to view or look at with side glances, as in fondness") me.

"I'll try to keep that in mind," I said. "Look up a little. What about the hair?"

He was still looking at my shirt. "It's great."

"David. You haven't even looked at it."

He tore his gaze from my chest and looked at my hair. His green eyes narrowed.

"It's black," he said.

I nodded. "Very good. Anything else? For instance . . . do you like it?"

"It's . . ." He stared at my head some more. "It's *very* black."

"Yes," I said. "It's called Midnight Ebony. Which led me to believe it might be black. Do you like it, is what I want to know."

David said, "Well, you aren't going to have to worry about anybody calling you Red anytime soon."

"I realize that," I said. "But do you think it looks good?"

"It looks . . ." David looked back down at my chest. "Great."

Wow. I wonder if Nike is aware of the power their shirts have over the eye sockets of people's boyfriends. At least mine, anyway. So much for being able to count on David for giving me an honest opinion on my new look. I guess I was going to have to wait for—

"What in God's name did you do to your hair?" Susan Boone looked horrified.

"I dyed it," I said, fingering a limp curl. I couldn't tell from her expression whether or not she approved. She mostly looked the way

29

Theresa and Lucy had . . . stunned. "Do you not like it?"

Susan bit her lower lip.

"You know, Sam," she said. "There are thousands of women who would kill for hair the color yours used to be. I hope that black isn't, er, permanent."

"Semi," I said weakly. The studio was filling up with life drawing students. Except for Rob, David's Secret Service agent—being the first son, David isn't allowed to go anywhere without being trailed by at least one Secret Service agent—I didn't recognize anyone.

Still, even though I didn't know any of the people in the Thursday class, they were all listening to our conversation—mine and Susan's.

Oh, they were pretending they weren't, fiddling around with their charcoal and drawing pads as they got settled.

But they were listening. You could tell.

"I just really needed a change," I said, trying to defend my—apparently bad—decision.

"Well, it's your head," Susan said with a shrug. Then she nodded at the army helmet David had given me last year, the one decorated with Wite-Out daisies, sitting on its shelf over the slop sink.

"Guess you won't be needing that anymore."

Which was true. I'd only worn it because Susan's pet crow, Joe, who roamed around loose during our drawing sessions, was morbidly obsessed with my red hair, and often dive-bombed me if I wasn't wearing protective head-gear. I eyed the evil bird, wondering if he was going to leave me alone now.

But Joe was busy preening himself on his perch, not paying the slightest bit of attention to anyone—least of all Midnight Ebony–haired little old me.

Yes! It worked! No more Joe to worry about.

"I think it looks good," David said, apparently finally able to register something other than the way my chest looked in my new shirt.

"Really?" I asked, hardly daring to get my hopes up. Finally, a positive response (from someone who'd actually seen it—Catherine's over-the-phone reassurances didn't count). "It's not too, um, Ashlee Simpson?"

David shook his head. "No way," he said. "Totally Enid from *Ghost World*."

Since this was exactly the look I'd been going for, I beamed.

"Thanks," I said. He really is the greatest

boyfriend ever. Even if he is slightly obsessed with my chest.

"All right, everyone," Susan said, coming to stand beside a low platform in the center of the room, which she'd covered with a brightly colored satin cloth. "Welcome to life drawing. As you can see, we have a couple of first timers here. This is David, Rob"—she pointed to David's Secret Service agent—"and Samantha."

Everyone murmured hello to us. I couldn't tell how many of them recognized David or me from TV. Maybe none of them. Maybe all of them. In any case, they were cool about it, not staring or giggling or being all Johnson Family Vacation about it or anything. Not that I'd expected them to, seeing as how they were all adults, and artists, besides. I mean, you sort of expect artists to behave with a modicum (SAT word meaning "a small quantity") more dignity than, say, your average, non-artist adult.

"Well, let's get started then." Susan called to someone who'd been hanging around the back of the room, "Terry? We're ready for you, I think."

Terry, a tall, thin guy in his twenties, came ambling over to the platform, wearing, for some reason, nothing but a bathrobe. I thought maybe this was on account of how we were supposed to be doing some kind of classical drawing.

Which was cool, because, hey, I didn't know we got to draw the models in *costume*.

This was going to be a lot more challenging, I knew, than drawing a piece of fruit, or cow horns. Terry's robe had a paisley pattern in it that was going to be hard to replicate. Especially in the places where the material folded.

I couldn't help giving a little squirm in eager anticipation. I know only a geek would be excited about drawing paisleys. But I *am* a geek. Or so I am informed on an almost daily basis by my peers, nearly every time I open my mouth in school, even if only to utter something innocuous, like that Gwen Stefani wrote the song "Simple Kind of Life" the night before No Doubt recorded it.

Then Terry climbed up onto the raised platform and I saw that it wasn't going to be hard to draw the paisleys on his robe at all. Because no sooner had I picked up my pencil than Terry tugged on the sash to his robe, and it fell into a puddle at his feet.

And underneath it, he was . . . well, completely naked.

Top ten things that have really and truly shocked me during my lifetime:

10. Gwen Stefani coming out with a solo album. I mean, I think it's great, don't get me wrong. But what about the rest of the band? I worry about them, is all. Except Tony, of course, since he's the one who broke her heart.

9. J.Lo and Ben's wedding getting called off. Seriously. I thought those two were made for each other. And what's with the Marc Anthony thing? I mean, he's shorter than she is, right? Not that there's anything wrong with that. But it's like she picked the one guy who P Diddy could beat up. And that's just wrong.

8. Lindsay Lohan starring in that Herbie the Love

Bug movie. Seriously. Why would they remake those movies? How could that ever have sounded like a good idea?

7. Passing German I–II.

6. Theresa's son Tito enrolling in technical college. And passing his first semester with flying colors.

5. The sight of my sister Lucy doing her own laundry.

4. Britney Spears marrying that back-up dancer of hers. Did she learn *nothing* from J.Lo?

3. Kristen Parks inviting me to her sixteenth birthday party at Six Flags Great Adventure (not that I went).

2. My boyfriend fixating on my chest so much that he wouldn't even notice my new hairstyle-slash-color.

And the number-one thing that really, truly shocked me:

1. That the first naked guy I ever saw was a total stranger.

2

$\mathcal{O}kay$, I've *seen* them before. Naked guys, I mean. On TV. In New York, when I go there for UN stuff, there's a whole public access channel devoted to naked guys.

And of course I've seen pictures of Michelangelo's statue of David. Not to mention all the classical art at the National Gallery, which is, you know. Mostly nudes.

And of course I've seen my dad naked. But only by accident, on the various occasions he's had to hop around, swearing, after getting out of the shower to find that Lucy has used up all the towels to dry her cashmere sweaters on, or whatever.

But the first naked guy not related to me that I ever saw *live* and *up close*? I totally didn't expect it to be someone I hadn't even known five minutes before.

To tell you the truth, I thought the first naked guy I'd ever see up close and personal like that would be my boyfriend, David.

Or so I'd been *hoping*. Boy, had *that* not worked out according to plan.

I looked around to see if anybody else was as surprised as I was to see Terry in the raw.

But everyone else was busily drawing away. Even David. Even Rob.

Excuse me, but what was up with *that*? Was I the only sane person in the room? Why was I the only one going, "Um, hello? Does anybody else notice the *naked guy* here? Or is it just me?"

Um, apparently so. No one else so much as blinked an eye. Just picked up their pencils and started sketching.

Okay, clearly I missed something somewhere.

Not knowing what else to do, I pretended to drop my eraser, then, when I was bending over to grab it, stole a quick peek at their drawing pads. David's and Rob's, I mean. I just wanted to see if they were . . . you know. Going to draw *all* of Terry. Or if maybe they were going to leave a polite blank space around his you-know-what. Because maybe that's what you were supposed to do. I didn't know. I mean, I couldn't even *say* it. How was I supposed to *draw* it?

I saw, however, that while they weren't making Terry's you-know-what the focal point of their drawings, both David and Rob had definitely roughed it in.

So, obviously, *they* didn't have a problem with drawing some naked dude.

Still, I have to admit, I was pretty weirded out by the whole thing. How come no one else was? Maybe it's easier to draw it if you actually own it. You know. The equipment.

And how did *Terry* even qualify to be the resident naked guy, anyway? He wasn't even good-looking. He was sort of skinny and had no muscle tone to speak of. He even had a tattoo of a heart with an arrow through it on his left bicep. He looked a lot like Jesus, actually, with his long blond hair and scruffy beard.

Only I haven't seen too many pictures of Jesus *naked*.

"Sam?"

Susan was speaking really softly—she tries to keep conversation to a murmur during class, making her voice lower than the radio, which was tuned to a soothing classical music station.

Still, softly as Susan had spoken, I jumped. Because classical music wasn't enough to soothe me, in my current state of hyper–naked guy awareness.

"WHAT?" I asked. For no reason at all, I started turning red. This is, of course, part of the curse of being red-headed. The tendency to blush for, like, no reason at all. I could feel my cheeks getting hotter and hotter. I wondered if, with my new black hair, my blush would be as noticeable as it used to be, back when my cheeks turned the same color as my bangs. I figured probably it was even *more* noticeable. The contrast, you know, of the black against the pink. Plus, you know, my eyebrows were still red. Although I had put black mascara on my eyelashes.

"Is there a problem? You're not drawing," was what Susan said softly, as she squatted next to my drawing bench.

"No problem," I said quickly. Maybe too quickly, since I spoke a little too loud, and David glanced my way, smiled briefly, then turned back to his drawing.

"Are you sure?" Susan glanced at Terry. "You've got a wonderful angle here." She picked up a piece of charcoal from the Baggie in front of me and sketched out a rough outline of Terry on my drawing pad. "You can really make out his inguinal ligament from here. That's the line from his hipbone to his groin. Terry's is quite defined. . . ."

"Um," I whispered uncomfortably. I had to say something. I *had* to. "Yeah. That's just it. I wasn't really expecting to *see* his inguinal ligament."

Susan looked away from her drawing and up toward me. She must have noticed something about my expression, since her eyes widened, and she said, "Oh. OH."

She got it. About Terry, I mean.

"But . . . what did you think I meant, Sam," she whispered, "when I asked if you'd be interested in joining my life drawing class?"

"That I'd be drawing from *life*," I whispered back. "Not a *naked guy*."

"But that's what life drawing means," Susan said, looking as if she were trying not to smile. "It's important for all artists to be able to draw the human form, and you can't do that if you can't see the muscle and skeletal structure beneath the skin because it's hidden under clothes. Life drawing has always meant nude models."

"Well, I realize that *now*," I whispered.

"Oh, dear," Susan said, not looking as if she wanted to smile anymore. "I just assumed . . . I mean, I really thought you knew."

I noticed that David was glancing our way. I didn't want him thinking there was anything wrong. I mean, the last thing I need is for my boyfriend to think I am freaked out by the sight of a naked guy.

"It's cool," I said, picking up my pencil and willing Susan to go away and leave me to blush in peace. "I get it now. It's all good."

Susan Boone didn't look as if she believed me, though.

"Are you sure?" she wanted to know. "You're all right?"

"I'm peachy," I said.

Oh my God. I can't believe I said peachy. I don't know what possessed me. The sight of a naked guy, and all I can think of to say is "I'm peachy"?

I don't know how I got through the rest of the class. I tried to concentrate on drawing what I *saw*, not what I *knew*, the way Susan had taught me to during our first lessons together. I still *knew* I was drawing a naked guy, but it helped when all I saw was a line going this way, and another line going that, and a shadow here, and another one there, and so on. By breaking Terry down into so many planes and valleys, I was able to render a fairly realistic and even kind of good (if I do say so myself) drawing of him.

When, at the end of the class, Susan asked us to put our drawing pads on the windowsill so we could critique each other's work, I saw that mine wasn't any better or worse than anybody else's. You couldn't, for instance, tell from mine that it was my first drawing of a naked guy.

Susan did say, though, that I hadn't done a very good job of fixing the subject of my drawing to the page. Which basically meant that my drawing was just of Terry, floating around, with no background to support him.

"What you've drawn here, Sam," Susan said, "is a fine representation of the parts. But you need to think of the drawing as a *whole*."

But I didn't take Susan's criticism about the parts versus the whole to heart, because I knew that it was a miracle I'd been able to draw anything at all, given my great naked guy–induced shock.

To make matters worse, later, as we were getting ready to go, Terry came up to me and was all, "Hey, I liked your drawing. Aren't you that chick who saved the president?"

Fortunately, he had put his jeans back on by then, so I was able to look him in the eye and go, "Yeah."

He nodded and said, "Cool. Thought so. That was, you know, brave. But, uh . . . what'd you do to your hair?"

"Just wanted a change," I said brightly.

"Oh," Terry said, appearing to think about that. "Okay. Well, that's cool."

Which isn't all that reassuring, if you think about it. I mean, seeing as how it was coming from someone who makes a living standing around without any clothes on.

Still, I guess I wasn't as cool in the studio as I thought I'd been, since on the way down to the car—David had offered to give me a lift home—he asked, barely able to contain the laughter in his voice, "So, what'd you think of Terry's . . . inguinal ligament?"

I nearly choked on the Certs I'd slipped into my mouth.

"Um," I said. "I've seen bigger."

"Really?" The laughter disappeared from David's voice. "His was pretty, um, pronounced."

43

"Not as big as some of the ones I've seen," I said, meaning the guys on Manhattan public access.

Then, seeing the stunned expression on David's face, I wondered if he knew that's what I meant—the guys I'd seen on TV, I mean.

Also, whether we were really talking about inguinal ligaments.

"I just hope it's a female model next time," Rob, the Secret Service agent, said, looking sadly down at his drawing pad. "Otherwise, I'm going to have a lot of explaining to do to the guys back at the office."

David and I laughed—nervously, in my case. I mean, I was still kind of shocked. I know that, as an artist, and all, I should see a naked body as just that—a naked body, the subject of the piece I was creating.

It was just that I couldn't help thinking about David's you-know-what and wondering if it was as big as Terry's (probably not, judging by his reaction to my inguinal ligament comment).

Which of course led me to wonder if I even *wanted* to see David's you-know-what. Up until today, I'd been pretty certain I did. You know. Someday.

Now, I wasn't so sure.

Of course, it wasn't like there'd been all that many opportunities for this kind of thing between us. Trying to find a private moment with the son of the leader of the free world is challenging, to say the least. Especially when there's always some guy with an earpiece lurking around.

Still, we did our best. There was my house, of course. My parents have a rule about boys in the bedrooms—i.e., they aren't allowed in them.

But my parents aren't *always* home. And Theresa's not usually around on weekends. When everyone else is gone—at one of Lucy's games, or Rebecca's qigong demonstrations, or whatever—David and I occasionally get a chance to engage in a little tonsil hockey, and sometimes more than that. Last Sunday, as a matter of fact, things between us got so, well, *heated* that we didn't even hear the front door slam. It was only because Manet, my dog, scrambled up from my bedroom floor to go greet whoever it was who'd come home early—Rebecca, dropped off from a friend's slumber party at the Smithsonian—that we didn't get caught in an extremely compromising position.

Not that I imagine Rebecca would have cared. When we came down the stairs, acting like we'd been doing nothing more exciting than homework, she just went, "Did you guys know that trans fats, like the ones found in Oreos, account for only about point five percent of daily calories for Europeans, as opposed to an estimated two point six percent for Americans, and that that's one reason why Europeans are so much skinnier than Americans, despite all the Brie they eat?"

Walking me to the door after dropping me off from wherever we'd been was really the *only* time David and I could count on the two of us being left alone for a few minutes . . . at least until Theresa or one of my parents realized we were out there and started flicking the porch light on and off.

I'm telling you, it's *hard* when your boyfriend is the president's son.

Anyway, as he walked me to my front door the evening of our first life drawing class, David pulled me into the shadows beneath the big weeping willow tree in the front yard—as was his custom—and pressed me up against the trunk as he kissed me.

This was also his custom. I must say, both

these customs delighted me very much.

Although that night, I was still sort of weirded out by the whole naked Terry thing and couldn't quite, you know. Get into it.

I think David could tell, since at one point he lifted his head and went, conversationally, "Did you really think that guy's inguinal ligament was small?"

"No," I said, to tease him. "Do you really like my hair?"

"Yes," he said to tease me back. "But I really, really like this shirt you have on. Do you want to go to Camp David with me for Thanksgiving? You can come if you promise to wear this shirt."

"Okay," I said—then slammed my head against the trunk of the tree as I whipped it back to look up at him. "Wait. WHAT did you just say?"

"Thanksgiving," he said, his lips moving up the side of my neck, toward my right ear lobe. "You've heard of it, surely. It's a national holiday, traditionally celebrated by ingesting large amounts of turkey and watching football—"

"I know what Thanksgiving is, David," I said. "What I mean is—Camp David?"

"Camp David is the official presidential

retreat away from the White House, located in Maryland—"

"Stop goofing around," I said. "I know what Camp David is. How did you talk your parents into letting you invite me there?"

"I didn't have to," David said with a shrug. "I just asked them if I could bring you, and they said sure. I'll admit that was before."

"Before what?"

"Before they saw what you did to your hair. But I'm sure they'll still let you come. So . . . want to?"

"Are you SERIOUS?" I couldn't believe he was being so jokey about it. Because this was big. I mean, *huge*. My boyfriend was asking me to go away with him. Overnight.

And okay, his parents were going to be there, and all. But even so, it could only mean one thing.

Couldn't it?

"Of course I'm serious," David said. "Come on, Sharona. It'll be fun. There's all sorts of stuff to do there. Horseback riding. Movies. Parcheesi."

Parcheesi? Was that some kind of weird boy code name for sex? Because that had to be what he was thinking we were going to do, right? I mean, have sex? Isn't that what couples who go away for the weekend together do?

"Don't even tell me you don't want to, Sharona," David was saying. "I know you do."

But how? How could he know I wanted to? Had I been giving off some I-want-to-have-sex vibe without even knowing it? Because I'm not sure I want to. Okay, sometimes I'm sure I want to, but not *most* of the time. And especially not *now*, having been forced to sit there and look at a naked guy for three hours. . . .

"You said you guys always go to your grandma's in Baltimore for Thanksgiving," David went on. "And that it's totally boring there. Right? So get out of it. And come to Camp David with me."

What should I say? I didn't know what to say!

"My parents will NEVER let me go away with you."

Seriously. That's what came blurting out of my mouth. Not "I'm not sure I'm ready yet, David," or "Are you talking about what I think you're talking about, David, or do you really mean Parcheesi as in . . . Parcheesi?"

No. None of *those* things. Instead, I just said

my parents wouldn't let me.

Which was sort of a comforting thought, actually. Especially in that it was true, and all.

"Sure they will," David said, in his usual unrufflable manner. "It's Camp DAVID. You'll be there with the PRESIDENT, and tons of Secret Service. Of course your parents will let you come. Besides, they trust you. Or at least they used to, before you did that to your hair."

"David. Don't joke. This is . . ." My heart was beating kind of hard, and not just because of frisson. "This is a really big step."

"I know," he said. "But we've been going out for more than a year. I think we're ready. Don't you?"

Ready for what? A weekend sleepover at Camp David, complete with turkey and Parcheesi? Or sex?

He *had* to be talking about sex. I mean, guys don't ask you to go to Camp David with them just for pumpkin pie and board games, right?

RIGHT?

"I don't know, David," I said hesitantly. "I mean . . . I think . . . I think I'm going to have to think about this. This is happening awfully fast."

But was it? I mean, really? Considering recent

events in the make-out department? Wasn't "a weekend at Camp David" just the next natural step?

"Come on," David said, his hand creeping up my shirt. "Say yes."

No fair. He was using his extremely talented fingers to manipulate my emotions. Or, er, not my emotions so much as my, um, appendages (SAT word meaning "body parts").

"Say you'll come," he whispered.

I would just like to say that it's very hard to know what the right thing to say is when a guy has his hand up your bra.

"I'll come," I heard myself whisper back.

How do I get myself into these things?

I mean, seriously.

Top ten places people commonly lose their virginity:

10. *Backseat of his car,* like Diane Court in
    Say Anything (although, considering it was
    with Lloyd Dobler, this probably wasn't so
    bad).

9. *Hotel after the prom.* This is such a cliché. So
   many girls think there's something romantic
   about losing it after the prom, apparently not
   realizing that the prom is just another thing the
   popular crowd invented to make the people in
   the non-popular crowd feel bad for not getting
   invited.

8. *Your parents' bed while they're away for the*

weekend. Ew. EW. It's your *parents'* bed, the place where you (possibly) were conceived. GROSS.

7. *HIS parents' bed while they're away for the weekend*. And it won't be at all embarrassing if his mother happens to find your Hello Kitty underwear at the bottom of her sheets.

6. *In a tent at summer camp*. Hello. It's a tent. EVERYONE CAN HEAR YOU.

5. *On a beach*. Sand. It gets everywhere.

4. *Anywhere out of doors at all*. One word: Bugs.

3. *His room*. Um, okay, have you ever happened to catch a whiff of his socks? His whole room smells like that. Seriously. Even if he happens to live in the White House. And he can't *tell*. He really can't. It's like his nostrils have gotten accustomed to it, the way yours have gotten accustomed to the smell of your own deodorant.

2. *Your room*. Oh, really? You're going to Do It in

front of Raggedy Ann and Mr. Snuffles? I think not.

And the number-one place people commonly lose their virginity:

1. *Camp David.* Well, okay, maybe this isn't the place where *most* people lose their virginity. But it's apparently the place where I'm going to lose mine.

3

The thing is, I have an ace in the hole (whatever that means. Something good, anyway).

And that ace is Mom and Dad.

Because NO WAY are Mom and Dad going to let me skip Thanksgiving at Grandma's to go away with my boyfriend.

Even to Camp David.

Even with the president.

Which means no sex. Or Parcheesi, as David apparently calls it.

I won't pretend like I am too upset about this. About my mom and dad not letting me go away with David. I mean, I'm not all that positive I even *want* to go. Okay, sure, I want to go when David's hands are under various articles of my clothing . . .

But the minute they aren't anymore, I have to admit, I'm not completely jazzed about the idea.

Because, let's face it, sex is an awfully big step. It completely changes your relationship. Or at least it does in the books Lucy likes to read, the ones she leaves lying around next to the bathtub that I occasionally pick up to peruse when I've run out of Vonnegut or whatever. In those books, whenever the girl and the guy start Doing It, that's it. That's *all* they do. So long going to the movies. So long going to dinner. All they ever do when they get together is . . . well, It.

Maybe that's just books and not how it is in real life. But how am I supposed to know for sure? It's just that I'm not sure I'm ready for that.

So if—although *when* is more like it—Mom and Dad say I can't go, it won't be the worst thing in the world. That's all I'm saying.

I dropped the bomb the minute I got back from life drawing. I decided that since Mom and Dad were just going to say no anyway, I might as well dispense with the beating-around-the-bush-and-dropping-of-subtle-hints thing. I mean, so what if they say no? David is going to have to learn to live with disappointment.

Mom and Dad were sitting there at the dining

room table with Lucy, who looked moderately upset, for some reason. Probably her favorite contestant on *American Idol* got voted off or something.

"Mom, Dad," I said, completely interrupting without remorse or preamble, "can I go to Camp David for Thanksgiving with, um, David"—I'd never realized until I said it just then that David has the same name as the presidential retreat. How weird is that? Plus, it sounds stupid to say—"and his parents?"

"Of course, honey," my dad said.

It was my mom who went, "Oh, God, Sam. What did you do to your hair?"

"I dyed it," I said. Meanwhile, my heart had totally skipped a beat. "What do you mean by '*Of course, honey,*' Dad?"

"Is it permanent?" my mom asked.

"Semi," I said to Mom. "Are you serious?" I asked Dad. "What about Grandma?"

"Grandma'll get over it," my dad said. Then he, too, became fixated on my hair. "What are you supposed to be?" he wanted to know. "One of those mango characters you're always reading about?"

"Manga," I corrected him. "What are you

saying, exactly? That I can go?"

"Go where?"

"To Camp David. With David. For Thanksgiving. Thanksgiving *weekend*. OVERNIGHT."

"I don't see why not," my mom said. "I assume his parents will be there? Well, fine. Next time you want to do something like this, Samantha, let me know beforehand. I'll make an appointment with my colorist. That over-the-counter stuff can't be good for your hair."

And just like that, it was over. They both turned their attention back to Lucy and whatever her glitch was . . . probably that she had a cheerleading practice that conflicted with some college tour they wanted her to take. They had been on her case about narrowing down some choices for college for a while now.

Leaving me to be all, um, hello? Remember me? Your other daughter? The one whose boyfriend just asked her to spend Thanksgiving weekend playing *Parcheesi* with him? And you said yes? Uh-huh, THAT daughter?

I couldn't believe it. *I couldn't believe it.* My parents were letting me go away for the weekend with my boyfriend.

And okay, you could see why they would, on

account of his dad being the president.

But just because your dad is the president doesn't mean you don't want to play *Parcheesi*. I mean, had they ever thought of that?

Apparently not. Apparently, my parents are the most clueless people on the face of the planet.

And now, thanks to them, it looked like I was going to Camp David for Thanksgiving, to get an up close and personal look at my boyfriend's inguinal ligament.

Okay. This isn't happening.

And yet, apparently, it is.

I was still reeling from the shock of it all when Lucy came flitting past my bedroom door a little while later. I had my headphones on—I was listening to *Tragic Kingdom*, in the hopes that Gwen's assurance that she's "just a girl in the world" would soothe my frazzled soul—so all I saw were Lucy's lips moving for a minute. When she didn't give up and go away after a while, I pulled my headphones off and went, in a voice unfriendly enough to startle my dog, Manet, from her sleep, "*What?*"

"That's what I was asking *you*," Lucy said. "Why do you look as if you just found out John Mayer died?"

Because in Lucy's world, if John Mayer died, people would *freak*. In *my* world if that happened? No one would notice.

"Um, because this year while you're helping Grandma light her pilgrim candle replicas of John and Priscilla Smith, I'm going to be losing my virginity to my longtime boyfriend at Camp David."

That's what I *want* to tell her.

But since I can't help thinking this isn't the wisest thing to confide to my sister, I just say the first thing that popped into my head, which is, "I don't know. I guess I'm just upset because . . . because . . . today, I saw my first, um, you-know-what."

I saw right away that I should have said something else. *Anything* else. Because this had the opposite effect of what I'd been hoping for—that Lucy would go away.

Instead, she came barreling all the way into my room, not even looking where she was going and knocking over my Hellboy action figures, which I had artfully set up along the top of my dresser to portray the Liz-on-the-sacrificial-slab scene.

"Really?" Lucy asked, all eager. "David's?

What'd he whip it out while he was kissing you good night out there just now? That is so gross. I hate when they do that."

"Um, no," I said, somewhat taken aback. Do guys actually *do* this? David certainly never has. But maybe only because he's too polite.

But it sounded like it's happened to my sister a *lot*. And she supposedly has a steady boyfriend! And okay, he's away at college, but still. What goes *on* at those parties she goes to, the ones at the popular people's houses? No wonder Kris Parks had embraced Right Way with so much vigor. She was probably psychologically scarred from guys whipping it out right and left in front of her.

"It was this guy named Terry's," I said. "He's a nude model Susan Boone made us draw."

This didn't seem to strike Lucy as any better than David having whipped it out.

"Ew!" she said. "You saw some skanky model guy's penis before you saw your own boy-friend's? That is sick."

Considering that's exactly how I'd been feel-ing a few hours before, it was funny that I heard myself replying, "Yeah, well, that's what life drawing is all about. Because you can't learn to

61

draw the human figure if clothes are obscuring the muscles and skeletal frame."

And then—I can't even begin to figure out why—I found myself confiding in her.

I know. Confiding in *Lucy*. I must have been out of my mind. Obviously ultra-cool Dauntra from Potomac Video would have been the logical person to turn to for guidance in this area. But no. I had to go and let my sister Lucy in on it. It was like my mouth just went running off by itself with no input whatsoever from my brain.

"But that's not all of it," I heard myself saying, to my horror. "Get this: David asked me to come to Camp David with him."

"Yeah, I know," Lucy said. "I was there when Mom and Dad said you could go, remember? Poor you. I mean, God, how boring. He couldn't take you to the mall, like a normal boyfriend?"

This was the perfect opportunity for me to drop it. I mean, considering Lucy clearly didn't understand a word I was saying.

But no. My mouth just kept on going.

"Lucy," I said. "I don't think you understand. *David asked me to spend the weekend with him at Camp David.*"

"Um," Lucy said. "Yes, I know. You said that

already. And I repeat, ew, how boring. I mean, what is there to do at Camp David? Ride horses? Throw rocks into some lake? I mean, I guess you two could paint, seeing as how you both like that kind of thing. But it's gonna be even more boring than Grandma's. I mean, it's not like there are any good outlet stores nearby."

"Lucy," I said, again. I couldn't believe she wasn't getting it. And I couldn't believe I was still trying to make her understand. What was I *doing*? Why was I telling *her*? "David asked me to come away with him. *For the weekend.* And Mom and Dad said yes."

Lucy sniffed. "Yeah, I noticed. You know, you're lucky they like him so much. Your boyfriend, I mean. They would never let me spend the weekend with Jack. But, of course, David's parents are going to be there."

"Yes," I said. It was hopeless. She was never going to understand.

And why should she? I mean, in Lucy's world, people like me—and let's face it, David—just don't, well, Do It. The idea that geeks might possibly have hormones, too, was very clearly an alien one to Lucy.

Or so I thought. I had basically given up on

the whole thing and was thinking to myself, *Well, actually, this is GOOD, since I didn't want her to know anyway*, when Lucy suddenly grabbed my wrist and, her Lancôme-lined eyes very wide, went, "Oh my God. You don't mean . . . Oh my God. You and David? And at CAMP DAVID?"

And that was that. She knew.

It was strange, but it was actually kind of a relief. Embarrassing, but a relief. Don't ask me why.

"Where else would you suggest?" I asked her, kind of sarcastically, to cover up my complete and utter mortification. "Under the bleachers?"

"Ew," Lucy said. "With all the wadded-up gum people have spat out? No." She had sunk down onto my bed—poking Manet, who was collapsed on top of my duvet, to get him to move over—and sat there, looking sort of stunned. "That is a really big step, Sam. Are you sure you're ready?"

"Part of me is," I heard myself admitting. "And part of me isn't. I mean, part of me really, really wants to, and part of me—"

"—is scared to death," Lucy concluded for me. "Well, don't be. Just make sure you use two methods of birth control," she went on, in the

64

same bossy way she always advises me not to wear my high-tops with a skirt or my legs will look fat. "I mean, he should wear a condom, but you should have a backup method, just in case. You have to start the Pill on the first Sunday of your period, and you just had yours last week, so even if you went to Planned Parenthood tomorrow, it wouldn't do you any good for Thanksgiving. I'd suggest spermicidal foam."

I just stared at her. With my mouth hanging open, I'm pretty sure.

But Lucy didn't seem to notice my shock.

"Don't buy the foam from any place in the neighborhood," she went on, briskly. "Someone we know might see you. And then it'll be all over school . . . and, in your case, all over the nightly news. You're bound to be recognized. God, saving David's dad was the worst thing you ever did. I mean, you can't do *anything* without everyone in the world wanting to know your business. Even with the hair. I mean, people can still tell it's *you*. It's just you with stupid-looking black hair. Look, do you want me to buy it for you?"

I just stared at her some more. Honestly, it was like I understood the words coming out of her mouth. I just couldn't believe she was *saying* them.

"You can't count on the guy taking care of it, Sam," Lucy said, apparently mistaking my stunned silence for indignation that she was poking her nose into my business. "Even a guy like David, who goes to that genius school. I mean, sure, he'll pick up some condoms. But condoms break. Sometimes they come off. Before they're supposed to, if you get my drift. You have to be . . . what's it called? Proactive. I'll pick something up for you after school tomorrow. Spermicidal foam is easy, you stick the applicator in like a tampon and just plunge it right in. You should have no problems."

"Ngrh," was all that came out of my mouth, due to my extreme freaked-outedness.

Lucy patted me on the head. Seriously. *She patted me on the head.* As if I were Manet.

"Don't worry about it," she said. "What are sisters for? I think you're doing the right thing, by the way. I mean, you guys have been going out forever, and David's a great guy, even if he is, you know, a little weird. What's with all the eighties bands T-shirts? And that whole art thing is a big yawn. But it's not like he has any choice. If he tried to bust out, even a little, it would be all over *Teen People*. And who needs that?"

"But—" I was pleased that I was at least capable of formulating words again. Sadly, I couldn't seem to make them go into a cohesive sentence. "But don't you—I mean, what about . . . Kris?"

Lucy blinked at me. "Kris who?"

"Um. Parks."

Don't even ask me why, at that particular moment, *she* popped into my head.

"What has SHE got to do with it?" Lucy wanted to know, wrinkling her perfect nose.

"Well," I said, "just that . . . I mean, you don't think that David and I should, um, wait?"

"Wait? For what?" Lucy looked generally puzzled.

"Well, like . . . you know." I shifted uncomfortably. "Um. Marriage?"

Lucy's eyes got very big. "Oh my God," she said. "What, you dye your hair, and you're Amish all of a sudden?"

"No." Now I felt even *more* uncomfortable. "It's just, you know. The slut factor, and all."

Lucy looked confused. "Since when does having sex with your boyfriend make you a slut?"

"Well," I said, coughing to clear my throat, which felt phlegmy all of a sudden. "You know. Kris. And, er, Right Way—"

67

Lucy laughed like this was the most hilarious thing she had ever heard. "Just stick to worrying about the Right Way for YOU, Sam."

Then she got up and said, "Well, it was nice having this little sex chat with you, but I have to go now. Mom and Dad got my SAT scores, and they are not what you would call pleased. They say I have to take them over. Oh, and get this: I have to get a tutor. *And* they're threatening to make me quit cheerleading so I'll have time to study. Can you believe it?" She shook her head sadly. "As if it matters what I got on my SATs when I want to be a fashion designer. You don't need good test scores to do *that*. Just a decent internship with Marc Jacobs. Anyway, I have to go call everyone I know now and tell them what total ruiners Mom and Dad are. See you."

Then she drifted off to her own room before I could say another word.

And just when I'd finally *thought* of some words to say, too. Because suddenly, I had some questions for her. Like, just how big is the average you-know-what, when it's, you know, in its inflated state?

And how long does the foam stay in after you, you know, Do It?

But then I thought maybe a blow-by-blow about Lucy's first time with Jack might be more than I could take, especially considering the fact that I, like just about everyone else in my family, wasn't so wild about Jack. He's a little more tolerable now that he's away at college and isn't always hanging around, expounding on his theories about how artists are so put upon and misunderstood by the rest of the world.

Which I will admit that at one time in my life I actually found quite intriguing.

But that was a dark period in my existence upon which I do not like to dwell. Not now that I'm in love with David, who never says things like, "The man is keeping me down" and "Society owes artists a living wage."

Which is one of the many reasons I love him . . . though it also helps that he's so enthusiastic about how I look in my Nike shirt.

I just wonder if I love him enough to let him see how I look with it off.

Top ten reasons why my sister Lucy has it *way* better than I do:

10. Because of saving the president, and all, I'm a celebrity, so whenever I do something really stupid—such as wear my shirt to school inside out, as I occasionally do before I've had enough caffeine to fully wake myself up—I can always count on a picture of it showing up in *People* or *Us Weekly* (Celebrities—They're just like us!).

9. While Lucy may have bombed the SATs, she never actually does anything as stupid as wearing a shirt inside out, so even if she *had* saved the president and was a national celebrity, they would never print pictures of her looking this dumb anywhere. Because this would never

happen to her. She always looks perfect everywhere she goes, no matter how early in the morning.

8. She is dating a teen rebel who owns a motorcycle, even if she is not allowed to ride on it with him, and gets to do cool stuff like go to the opening night of a performance art piece featuring a punk rock band throwing pieces of raw meat at a screen on which are projected various photos of world leaders. Whereas I am dating the president's son, so I get to do fun things like go to the opening night of *Tosca* at the Kennedy Center with the various world leaders themselves, which isn't anywhere near as fun.

7. When I get my photo in *Us Weekly* almost every single week, wearing an inside-out shirt or whatever, it's usually right next to Mary-Kate and Ashley. If Lucy were the celebrity, and not me, you can bet her picture would be next to someone way cooler, like Gwen Stefani.

6. Tons of designers send me free clothes, begging me to wear them instead of my inside-out shirts,

so that their clothes will be in *Us Weekly*. Except of course I have to send most of them back, because my parents won't let me wear leather bustiers and, also, unlike Lucy, I do not have the chest to hold up a bustier. Lucy would totally get to keep them.

5. My boyfriend apparently calls sex Parcheesi. I don't know what Lucy's boyfriend calls it. But I'm guessing probably not that.

4. Lucy can figure out sales tax in her head. Oh, and she can do a back handspring. All I can do is draw a naked guy. And apparently, I can't even do that very well, since I concentrate on the parts and not the whole.

3. Mom and Dad totally like—and trust—my boyfriend. Lucy's boyfriend? Not so much. So they spend hours arguing with her about him, telling her she could do better, et cetera. Mom and Dad basically ignore me.

2. I have only one friend—my best friend, Catherine, who is so sweet and sensitive I can't even tell her about my boyfriend possibly wanting to have

sex with me over Thanksgiving weekend on account of it would freak her out since she doesn't even *have* a boyfriend anymore (unless you count the one in Qatar, which I don't), whereas Lucy has nine million friends who she can tell *anything* to because they are completely shallow and have no emotions. Like cyborgs.

And the number-one reason why Lucy has it *way* better than I do:

1. She's clearly already lost her virginity and has put it behind her, since it was obviously no big deal to her. It is a *huge* deal to me, however, which means I will probably be stuck with it (my virginity) until my thirties, or death, whichever comes first.

4

"*Wait*, so, what did it look like?" Catherine wanted to know.

I couldn't believe she was so curious. I mean, I *could*. But I also couldn't. Because I really didn't want to talk about it.

"It looked like a penis," I said. "What do you think? I mean, you've seen them before. You used to go skinny dipping at the shore with your brothers when you were little, you said."

"Yeah, sure," Catherine said. "But that was before they got, you know. Hair down there."

"Okay," I said. "Gross."

"Well, it's true. Seriously. How big was it?"

I was starting to be sorry I'd brought it up. I'd only done so because she'd asked how my life drawing class had gone. I'd thought to share with her the true meaning behind the words "life drawing."

Now I wished I hadn't.

"It was average, I guess," I said. "I mean, it's not like I have a lot of experience in that department."

"I'm just glad I don't have one," Catherine said with a delicate shudder. "I mean, can you imagine, having it dangling there, all the time? How do they even ride bikes?"

"Sam?" Trust Kris Parks to choose that moment, of all the moments in the world, to sidle up to us where we stood in the lunch line and go, "Got a minute?"

Kris is not exactly my favorite person. And up until I became a semi-celebrity, the feeling was mutual.

But then I was on the six o'clock news a couple of times, and Kris decided I was her new best friend. I guess the fact that I'm dating the president's son outweighs the fact that I don't own a stitch of Lilly Pulitzer. Which, in Kris's book, makes you one of those Untouchables Rebecca and I learned about on *National Geographic Explorer*.

"Listen, I was wondering if we could count on you to help us set up the gym next week," Kris said with a simper (SAT word meaning "to smile in a silly, affected, or conceited manner"). "You know, for the town hall meeting. . . ."

"Yeah, sure," I said, to make her go away.

"Swell," Kris said. Trust Kris to say something like "swell." It was almost as bad as me saying something like "I'm peachy" upon seeing my first you-know-what. "We can really use the help. So far the only people who've volunteered are, you know, the student council members. And Right Way, of course. It's really embarrassing. I mean, that the president is going to be announcing this important new program from right here in our own school, and most of the kids in this school are so apathetic about it. I really hope he doesn't think we're *all* like that. The president, I mean. I really want to make us look good in front of him. And Random Alvarez. I mean, he's just so hot—" Then she got a good look at my head. "What happened to your—" She broke off and bit her lip. "Never mind."

"My hair?" I reached up to finger it. "I dyed it. Why? Don'tcha like it?"

I knew Kris didn't like my hair. Preps like Kris aren't into Midnight Ebony. I was just torturing her for the fun of it.

"Oh, no, it's really nice." Kris seemed to

recover herself. "It's permanent?"

"Semi," I said. "Why?"

"No reason," Kris said with a bright smile. "Looks great!"

I knew Kris was lying, and not just because her lips were moving. I had given myself a fully objective examination in the bathroom mirror just that morning, and I knew for a fact that Lucy was right: My new black hair looked stupid. Maybe if I had dyed my eyebrows to match, it might not have looked so bad.

But I hadn't done it as a fashion statement so much as a *statement* statement . . . that statement being, "Say so long to red-haired, goody-two-shoes, president-saving Samantha Madison, and say hello to life-drawing, possibly-soon-not-to-be-a-virgin Sam."

Of course, the fact that I'd dyed my hair *before* my first life drawing lesson, and then decided to rid myself of my virginity (possibly), was just symbolic of how far I'd come from the pre-dye, red-headed me.

"This Return to Family initiative of the president's," Kris went on, studiously ignoring my hair. "I hope you'll tell him how excited we all are about it here at Adams Prep, and that we're behind him one hundred and ten percent. I mean, family is the most important thing."

"Yeah," I said. "Well, who isn't pro-family?" That's what I said. But inside my head, I was going, *Why won't you die, Kris Parks? Why?*

"Maybe you'd be interested in coming to a Right Way meeting sometime?" Kris glanced at Catherine, as if aware for the first time that I wasn't standing there alone. "You and your, uh, friend."

Kris knows perfectly well what Catherine's name is. She was just being what she is, a preppy uber-snob.

Which she illustrated a second later by going, as a girl in an Adams Prep dance team uniform walked by in her flippy purple skirt, "Oh my God, did you hear about Debra Mullins? She supposedly hooked up with Jeff Rothberg under the bleachers after the Trinity game last week. She's *such* a slut." Then she added, cheerfully, to me, "Well, see you in the gym Monday!"

"Oh, we'll be there," I said, just to get Kris to leave.

It worked. She left us to order our double cheeseburgers in peace.

"God, I hate her," Catherine said.

"Tell me about it."

"No, I mean, I *really* hate her."

"Welcome to my world."

"Yeah, but at least she sucks up to you. On account of David. She'd never call *you* a slut. I mean, if you and David ever, you know, hooked up. And she found out." Then, Catherine added, with a laugh, "Like that's ever going to happen."

I didn't know which Catherine found more unlikely—the prospect of David and me ever having sex, or Kris finding out about it. I wasn't about to let her know that the former was more imminent (SAT word meaning "threatening to occur immediately; near at hand; impending") than she might expect. Not because I didn't trust her to keep it a secret. I'd trust Catherine with my life.

It was just that I still wasn't sure what I was going to do. About Thanksgiving, I mean. I hadn't had a chance to tell David yet that my mom and dad had actually said yes to my spending the weekend with him at Camp David.

Which I was still sort of mad about. Their saying yes, I mean. It was so *obvious* that they'd only said yes because they'd been distracted by Lucy and her SAT score situation. I mean, God forbid Mom and Dad should pay attention to *me* for a change. As usual, the middle child was getting the short end of the stick, attention-wise, in the Madison household.

Although I guess I couldn't *totally* blame Lucy for their saying yes. The fact is, my parents have this perception that I'm the Good Kid. You know, the one who, yeah, might try to dye her hair black, but who ultimately is going to throw herself on an assassin to save the president. Nobody worries too much about a kid like that. A kid like *that* would never do something as reprehensible as sleep with her boyfriend over Thanksgiving weekend.

It would *so* serve my parents right if I became an unwed teen mother.

Still, I wasn't about to mention any of this to Catherine. She has enough to deal with, what with her mom not letting her wear pants to school—seriously, she has to wear below-the-knee skirts, even in P.E.—and the mockery this brings with it. I'm not about to add to Catherine's troubles the fact that her best friend is considering losing the big V.

Besides, it isn't anybody's business, really. Anybody's but my own.

"Whoa," Dauntra said, when I burst through the door to Potomac Video with just a minute to spare before my after-school shift started. "You did it!"

I didn't know what she was talking about at first. I thought she meant that I'd decided to have sex with my boyfriend, and wondered how she'd known. Especially since I hadn't decided any such thing. Yet.

Then I remembered my hair.

"Yeah," I said. I have to admit, her reaction—which was actually admiring—made all the *What did you do to your hair?*'s I'd gotten in school today totally worth it. Around Potomac Video—just like around my own home—I am perceived as somewhat of a goody-goody. I mean, I'm the girl who saved the president, the girl who doesn't *need* that $6.75 an hour to pay for childcare or whatever. I'm considered something of a freak around there.

Until, of course, I dyed my hair. Now, I was cool.

I hoped.

Because the clerks at Potomac Video? They're *way* cool.

Especially Dauntra, with whom, along with Stan, the night manager, I work on Friday nights. Her motto (taped to her employee locker): *Question authority*. Her favorite movie: *A Clockwork Orange*. Her political party: not the same as David's dad. In fact, one of the first things she ever asked me was, "Has it ever occurred to you that if you had just let him get shot, you might have spared us all a lot of grief?"

And while this might be true, I don't think even Dauntra could have stood there and just watched someone point a gun at someone else, no matter how different her political views were from that person's. Especially, as I'd pointed out to her, considering the fact that, much as people might dislike the president—and judging from the latest polls, people disliked him very, very much—I knew someone who loved him a lot. Namely his son, my boyfriend, David. No matter how much he might disagree with some of the things his dad has done during his administration, David's affection for his father never wavered.

And for that reason—not to mention the fact that, really, I'd had no choice in the matter. I hadn't so much acted that day as *reacted*—I was glad I'd done what I had.

"Now *that*," Dauntra said with approval, nodding at my hair, "is what I'm talking about."

"You like it?" I threw my backpack into my employee locker. Later, before I leave, Stan will go through it, to make sure I haven't ripped off any DVDs. My backpack, I mean. Even though I was the store's token goody-goody, everyone's bag gets searched before they leave. Even mine. It's the Potomac Video way.

Although certain of its employees are trying to change that.

"I love the black," Dauntra said. "It makes your face look thinner."

"I don't know if thin-faced was the look I was going for," I said. "But thanks."

"You know what I mean." Dauntra, whose hair is two-toned, Midnight Ebony and Pink Flamingo, fiddled with her eyebrow ring. "What did your parents say? Did they lose it?"

"Not really," I said, ducking back behind the counter. "They barely noticed, actually."

Dauntra made a disgusted noise.

"God, what are you going to have to do to get their attention, anyway?" she wanted to know. "Have a baby at the prom?"

"Um," I said, choking a little on the diet Dr Pepper I'd bought at the convenience mart next door before my shift. Because, you know, considering recent events, my having a baby at the prom isn't *totally* out of the realm of the possible. "Yeah. Ha. That would probably do it, all right. But, you know, there's something to be said for maintaining a low profile. Right now they're all over Lucy, on account of her SAT scores."

Dauntra's look of disgust deepened. "When are people going to get that that stupid test doesn't mean anything? I mean, what does it measure? How well you paid attention in class the past decade of your life? Please. Like *that* can tell a college admissions office anything about how well you're going to do for the next four years while you're at their school."

Dauntra, whose parents kicked her out of the house one night after she turned sixteen and got an eyebrow ring (and a twenty-year-old boyfriend), is currently studying graphic design at a community college. She'd dumped the boyfriend, but kept the eyebrow ring, and opted out of the whole SAT trap by refusing to take them, or to enroll in a school that required them.

Dauntra has a lot of opinions like that. I actually think that she and Lucy's boyfriend, Jack, have a lot in common that way.

"So what'd the 'rents do?" Dauntra wanted to know. "About your sister?"

"Oh," I said. "They're making her get a tutor. And cut back on the cheerleading to make time for it. The tutoring, I mean."

"Typical," Dauntra said. "I mean, them playing into the whole sick fallacy that those scores mean anything. Although if it means your sister spends less time in a miniskirt, undermining the feminist cause, I guess it's a good thing."

"Totally," I said.

I thought about asking Dauntra what she thought I should do about David and the whole Thanksgiving thing. I mean, she is more experienced than I am—probably more than Lucy, too. I figured the advice from a woman of the world like Dauntra might be really valuable, not to mention insightful.

Only I couldn't really figure out how to bring it up, you know? Like, was I just supposed to go, "Hey, Dauntra. My boyfriend asked me to spend Thanksgiving with him at Camp David, and you know what that means. Should I say yes or no?"

Somehow, I just couldn't bring myself to do it. So instead, I asked her, conversationally, "So, how's the battle of the backpack going?"

Dauntra glanced darkly in Stan's direction. "Stalemate," she said. "He said if I didn't like it, I could go work at McDonald's."

Dauntra's convinced that the video store's policy of having a manager go through employee backpacks before allowing them to leave after their shift is unconstitutional—even though I'd asked my mom about it, and she'd said, technically, it wasn't. Dauntra refused to believe this, but it's cool she even cares. Some people I know— well, okay, Kris Parks, to be exact—only *pretend* to care about issues because doing so looks good on their college applications.

"I was thinking about pouring Aunt Jemima all over the inside of my JanSport," Dauntra went on, "so when Stan reaches inside it tonight, he gets a big handful of syrup. But I don't want to ruin a perfectly good backpack."

"Yeah," I said. "I can see how that might hurt more than help. Besides, it isn't Stan's fault, necessarily. He's just doing his job."

Dauntra narrowed her eyes at me. "Yeah," she said. "That's what all the Nazis said in their own defense after World War Two."

I didn't think searching someone's backpack for stolen DVDs was quite the same as killing seven million people, but I didn't figure Dauntra would appreciate me mentioning that out loud.

"Anyway," she said, changing the subject, "how was that new art class? The life drawing one?"

"Oh," I said. "Kind of, um, startling." I still didn't feel comfortable bringing up the David thing, so I just said, "Did you know life drawing meant nudes?"

Dauntra didn't even look up from the manga she'd cracked open over the register's keyboard.

"Yeah. Of course."

"Oh," I said, slightly let down. "Well, I didn't. So I got to see my first—you know."

That got her attention.

"The nude model was a GUY?" She looked up from the comic book—well, it was really a comic novel, or graphic novel. I should start trying to get the terminology correct, since someday I hope to write and illustrate mangas of my own. "I thought nude models were always women."

"Not always, I guess," I said.

"You know, some guy dropped his pants in front of me on the Metro the other day," Dauntra said incredulously, "for free. I had to call the cops. And, like, this Susan Boone lady, she pays some guy *money* to do it?"

"Yeah," I said.

Dauntra shook her head in disbelief. "Did you feel violated? Because whenever a guy shows me his goods when I'm not interested in seeing them, I feel violated."

"It wasn't really like that," I said. "I mean, you know. It was art."

"Art." Dauntra nodded. "Sure. I can't believe a guy gets paid to show off his goods, and people call it art."

"Well, not the showing-off-his-goods part," I said. "But the drawings we make of it."

Dauntra sighed. "Maybe I should take up being a nude model. I mean, you get paid just to sit there."

"Naked," I pointed out.

"So what?" Dauntra shrugged. "The human form is a thing of beauty."

"Excuse me." A tall guy in a beret—no, really, a French beret, although he didn't happen to look French—approached the counter. "I believe you're holding a film for me. The name is Wade, W-A-D—"

"Yeah, it's right here," I said quickly. Because the guy in the beret is a regular, and even though I'd only been working at Potomac Video for two months, I knew that if you didn't head off Mr. Wade at the pass, he'd go on for as long as he could about his film collection, which is extensive, and mostly in black and white.

"Ah, yes," he said, when I showed him the DVD we'd been holding for him. "*The Four Hundred Blows*. You know it, of course?"

"Of course," I said, even though I had no idea what he was talking about. "That will be fourteen seventy-nine."

"One of Truffaut's finest," Mr. Wade said. "I have it on video, of course, but it's really the kind of film you can't own enough copies of—"

"Thank you," I said, bagging the DVD, then handing him the bag.

"A truly powerful work," Mr. Wade went on. "A masterful piece of suspense . . ."

"Just how big were the guy's goods, anyway?" Dauntra asked me, in a sweetly innocent voice.

Mr. Wade, looking suddenly alarmed, snatched up his bag and fled the store.

"Come again," Dauntra called after him,

and the two of us practically collapsed, we were laughing so hard.

"What was that all about?" Stan, the night manager, came out from behind the Westerns and eyed us suspiciously.

"Nothing," I said, wiping tears of laughter from my eyes.

"Mr. Wade was so excited to get his new DVD, he wanted to rush home to watch it, that's all," Dauntra said, in a convincingly sincere voice.

Stan looked as if he didn't believe us.

"Madison," he said, "some anime fans were in here earlier and got the *Neon Genesis Evangelion*s all out of order. See what you can do about that, will you?"

I said I would, and ducked out from behind the counter to go check on the anime section.

Later, after the post-dinner rush, Dauntra was reading another manga while I pulled out the materials the White House press secretary had given me the other day to prepare me for my big speech, and was going over them.

"What *is* all that?" Dauntra wanted to know.

"Stuff I gotta talk about on MTV next week," I said. "At the town hall meeting at my school."

Dauntra looked as if there were a bad taste in her mouth. "That stupid Return to Family thing?"

I blinked at her. "It's not stupid. It's important."

"Yeah," Dauntra said. "Whatever. God, Sam. Don't you ever resent it, being used that way?"

"Used? How'm I being used?" I asked.

"Well, the president's using you," Dauntra said, "to spoon-feed his fascist new program to America's youth."

"Return to Family isn't fascist," I said. I didn't mention that, even if I didn't approve of it, I couldn't exactly quit being teen ambassador. Not without making things exceedingly awkward with my boyfriend's parents. "It's a program that encourages families to spend more time together. You know, to take a night off from soccer practice and TV and just sit around and talk."

"Yeah," Dauntra said darkly. "On the *surface*, that's all it is."

"What are you talking about?" I waved the papers I was holding. "I've got it all right here. That's what it is. The president's Return to Family initiative, to—"

"—encourage people to take a night off from mindless sitcoms and talk to one another," Dauntra finished for me. "I know. But that's just the part of the Return to Family plan they're *telling* you about. What about the rest of it? The parts they don't want you to know about . . . yet?"

"You," I said, "are paranoid. You've seen that Mel Gibson movie too many times."

Conspiracy Theory is one of our favorite movies to watch in the store. Stan hates it, because whenever Mel and Julia Roberts kiss, or are about to, Dauntra and I find ourselves incapable of doing anything but stare at the screen.

"Well, didn't he turn out to be right?" Dauntra asked. "Mel, I mean? There *was* a conspiracy." She glanced over at the two-way mirror that separated us from the back office. The two-way mirror is supposedly there so Stan or whoever is back there can catch shoplifters. But Dauntra is convinced it's really so the owners or whoever can spy on the employees. "It's never good," Dauntra added, "when the government starts putting its nose in our personal business, like how much time we spend together as families. Trust me on this one."

I turned back to my paperwork with a sigh. I love Dauntra, and all, but sometimes I'm not so sure she's all there, if you know what I mean. Who has time to worry about the government and what it's up to when there are so many real problems out there? Like my boyfriend, for instance, apparently thinking we are going to have sex over Thanksgiving weekend.

I thought once more about asking Dauntra, you know, about David and me, and what she thought about the possible Turkey Day divestment of my virginity.

The thing is, I knew she'd be all for my losing it. I also knew that, if I told her, it would help dispel my good-girl image at the store, an image I couldn't quite seem to shake, even with my newly dyed hair.

But telling my sister was one thing. Telling my fellow Potomac Video employees was something else entirely. I mean, in spite of my affection for *Conspiracy Theory*, I don't actually believe in conspiracies . . . like that Dauntra is really a spy for *Us Weekly* or whatever, and the minute I let some intimate detail of my relationship with the first son slip, she's going to report it.

But still. Maybe Dauntra was right about one

thing: It's better not to let the government—or your fellow employees at Potomac Video—put their noses in your business. Some things really are better left private.

At least, that's what I thought then. Funny how quickly your opinion on that kind of thing can change.

Top ten Potomac Video employee picks:

10. *Fight Club*: A disillusioned man meets a stranger who introduces him to a new way of life. Brad Pitt, Edward Norton, 1999. Shirtless Brad, disillusionment, and big explosions. What could be bad about it?

9. *To Kill a Mockingbird*: A lawyer in the Depression-era South defends a black man falsely accused of rape and teaches his son and daughter not to be prejudiced. Gregory Peck, Mary Badham, 1962. Two words: Boo Radley. Need I say more? I didn't think so.

8. *Heathers*: Popular girl meets a rebel who shows her how to teach the snobby girls at her school a lesson. Christian Slater, Winona Ryder, 1989.

Anyone who tries to say this isn't how high school really is, is a liar. Also contains the immortal line: *"I love my dead gay son."*

7. *Donnie Darko*: High school boy is haunted by visions of a giant rabbit. Jake Gyllenhaal, Patrick Swayze, 2001. Okay, I don't understand it. But I love it.

6. *Napoleon Dynamite*: A high school outcast helps a new boy run for student body president, while wooing the girl of his dreams. Jon Heder, Efren Ramirez, 2004. Best dance scene of any movie, ever.

5. *Saved!*: Girl at religious school is ostracized by peers. Jena Malone, Mandy Moore, 2004. This movie closely tied with *Camp* for pure hilarity.

4. *Dogma*: Two renegade angels try to get back into heaven. Linda Fiorentino, Matt Damon, 1999. Alanis Morissette plays God. Never has any role been cast so aptly.

3. *Secretary*: A secretary begins an unorthodox romance with her employer. Maggie Gyllenhaal, James Spader, 2002. Disturbing in a way that

makes you go *Hmmm*.

2. *I'm the One That I Want*: Margaret Cho's 1999 stand-up comedy routine. Margaret Cho, 2000. Should probably be required viewing for all humans.

And my number-one top ten Potomac Video employee pick:

1. *Kill Bill* Volumes 1 and 2: A hired assassin seeks vengeance when she, in turn, is attacked and left for dead. Uma Thurman, David Carradine, 2003/2004. Why do people even bother to keep making movies when *Kill Bill* exists? *Kill Bill* has it all. You don't have to watch anything else, really.

5

When I got home from work that night, it was to find a sight so confusing that for a minute, I thought I had entered the wrong house. I almost turned around and went back out again. That's how bizarre I found what I was seeing.

Lucy was sitting at the dining room table with a bunch of books spread out in front of her.

On a Friday night. A *Friday* night. Lucy is *never* home on Friday night. Up until recently, she's always either been at a game or out with Jack, who travels down almost every weekend to see her. Lately, of course, she's been working the Friday night shift at Bare Essentials, over in the mall.

But not this Friday night. This Friday night, she was going over SAT vocabulary words with—and this was the part that had me convinced I had the wrong house, the wrong sister, the wrong everything—Harold Minsky.

There are a lot of places I might have expected to see Harold Minsky. Potomac Video, for one, in the very anime section I'd just spent an hour organizing. Or possibly the sci-fi shelves. I would definitely have expected to see him in the computer lab at school, where he practically lives, in his capacity as teacher's assistant to Mr. Andrews, the computer lab supervisor.

I wouldn't have been at all surprised to see Harold in the manga aisle at our local Barnes and Noble, or standing in front of Beltway Billiards, where he and his friends spend hours attaining high scores on Arcade Legends.

But I can't say I expected, in a million years, ever to find Harold Minsky in my house . . . much less sitting across the dining room table from my sister Lucy.

"Waggish," Lucy was saying thoughtfully as I walked in. "You mean, like a dog?"

Harold said, in a bored voice, "No." Then, when there was no reply from my sister, he prompted, "It's an adjective."

"Waggish." Lucy looked up at the ceiling, as if

expecting the vocab fairy to tumble down from the chandelier and help her out. Instead, she noticed me standing in the doorway with my mouth sagging open.

"Oh, hi, Sam," she said brightly. "Do you know Harold? Harold, this is my sister Samantha. Samantha, this is Harold. You know. From school."

I did know. Harold was my computer lab TA. I said, "Uh, hi, Harold."

Harold nodded at me, then turned his bespectacled head (how could it not be, when his parents had named him Harold?) back toward Lucy. What could they have been thinking, by the way? Didn't they know that naming a kid Harold was a self-fulfilling prophecy, guaranteed to turn him into all that the name stood for: glasses, a crop of weedish brown hair that was badly in need of cutting, an unsteady gait stemming from a frame that had shot up six inches over the previous summer, making him one of the tallest guys in school not actually on the basketball team, and an orange Hawaiian shirt, the tail of which flopped out from the waistband of his too-short Levi's?

"Come on," he said in a no-nonsense tone

that I'm sure no male member of the species had ever used on my sister before in her life. "You know this one. We just went over it."

"Waggish," Lucy said obediently. Then, to me, added, "Oh, I got that thing for you, Sam. That thing we talked about the other night? It's on your bed."

At first I didn't know what she was talking about. Then, when she winked slowly, it hit me—and I blushed. Deeply.

Fortunately, Harold was too caught up in getting my sister to come up with a definition for waggish (SAT word meaning "mischievous in sport; roguish in merriment or good humor; frolicsome") to notice me.

"Lucy," he said severely, "if you aren't even going to try, I see no point in wasting my time and your parents' money——"

"No, no, wait," Lucy said. "I know this one. Really, I do. Waggish. Doesn't it mean 'happy'? Like, the football victory left him feeling waggish?"

I had to pass by the living room to get upstairs. My parents were both sitting in there, pretending to read. But I knew they were listening to Lucy and her new tutor.

"Hi, honey," my mom said, when she saw me. "How was work?"

"Workish," I said, keeping my head ducked in the hope that she wouldn't notice my still-bright-red cheeks. "How long's *that* been going on?" I jerked a thumb over my shoulder, toward the dining room.

"Tonight's their first session," Mom said. "I called the school, and they told me this Harold is the best SAT prep tutor they've got. Do you know him? Do you think he'll be able to help her?"

"Well," I said slowly. "If anyone can, I'd guess it would be Harold."

"They tell me he's a shoo-in for Harvard," my mom said. "All the Ivies, actually."

"Yeah," I said. "That sounds like Harold, all right."

"I asked for a female tutor," my mom said, making sure to lower her voice so that Lucy and Harold couldn't overhear her, "because I didn't want there to be any . . . romantic complications. You know how boys can be about your sister. But when I saw Harold in action with her, I knew he'd be perfect. It's almost as if he doesn't even realize she's . . . well, the way she is."

It was nice of my mom not to come right out and say what we were all thinking: That Lucy is so gorgeous, guys on the street routinely fall in love with her on sight, and often trail after her, holding out scraps of paper with their cell phone numbers scrawled on them, which Lucy always politely takes, then deposits without a second thought in her bedroom trash can when she cleans out her purse every evening.

"Um," I said. "Yeah. That'd be Harold, all right. He doesn't go in for that popularity stuff." Or girls much, really. Unless they're named Lara Croft and live inside a PlayStation.

"I don't care if he falls in love with her," my dad said, roughly turning a page of the newspaper he was holding. "So long as he gets her score up, I'll be happy."

"Oh, Richard," my mom said. "Not so loud. David called while you were at work, Sam. He said to call him back when you get a chance."

"Huh," I said. "Great."

Only I didn't mean great. I actually meant the opposite of great. Because I knew why he was calling. To find out what Mom and Dad had said. To find out whether or not we were going to get together over Thanksgiving to play Parcheesi.

And the truth is, I've never actually been the hugest fan of board games.

What would he do, I wondered, if I said no? No, I don't want to go to Camp David with you for Thanksgiving, David. Would he dump me? I mean, if I just came out and told him that while he might think we're ready for sex, I'm not so sure?

No. No way. David's not that kind of guy. For one thing, he's a total nerd—I mean, card carrying, with his vintage Boomtown Rats T-shirts, Converse high-tops, and long, strictly sci-fi related TiVo To Do list. And let's face it, nerds simply don't dump their girlfriends for not putting out, the way jocks seem to. Or so I've heard, not actually being acquainted with any jocks.

And for another thing, I know David really loves me. I know that because of the way he can be making fun of my hair one minute, and nibbling on my neck, telling me how hot he thinks I look in my new Nike shirt the next. I also know because I'm the last person he speaks to every night before he goes to sleep (he never forgets to call my cell. . . . if I'm already asleep—or pretending to be, like I was last night—he leaves a message) and the first person he calls when he wakes up (not that I always answer, since I am not fit to be spoken to before my morning diet Dr Pepper).

And he doesn't call just because he feels like he has to or I'll have a breakdown—the way Lucy does with Jack—but because . . . well, he wants to.

No, David's not going to dump me if I tell him I'm not ready. He loves me. He'll wait.

I think.

Besides, if he *did* dump me, the press would eat him alive. Not to sound braggy, but I am quite beloved by the American people for saving the life of their leader.

Although that was pre–dye job. Who knows how Margery in Poughkeepsie is going to feel about me once she sees my new apparently Ashlee Simpson–esque do?

"This Return to Family initiative David's father is promoting," my mom said, breaking in on my musings about my sex life—or lack of one. "I really like the idea. Sometimes I feel like I never get to see you kids, you're all so busy."

I just stared at her, completely shocked.

"Whose fault is that?" I practically yelled. "This part-time job thing wasn't exactly MY idea, you know."

My dad lowered his paper again. "It's important for you kids to learn the value of a—"

"Yeah, yeah," I interrupted my dad. "A dollar. I know." Like anything even costs a dollar anymore. "Speaking of which, did Lucy switch shifts, or what? Why is she home so early? Usually she doesn't get back from the mall until ten."

I noticed the glance my mom and dad exchanged. Don't think I didn't.

"We decided that, given Lucy's SAT score, she needs to devote more time to her schoolwork, and less to her social life and work schedule," my mom said lightly.

It took me a minute to figure out what she meant. Then, when I finally did, my jaw dropped all over again.

"Wait a minute," I cried. "She gets to quit her job just because she bombed the SATs? That's not fair!"

"Shhh, Sam." My mom glanced nervously toward the dining room. "Lucy's very upset about having to give notice at Bare Essentials. You know how much she loved that employee discount—"

"So if my grades start to slip," I demanded,

"can I quit Potomac Video?"

"Sam!" My mom gave me a reproachful look. "What a thing to say. You love your job. You're always talking about your little Donna friend, and how cool she is—"

"Dauntra."

"Dauntra, I mean. Besides, you can handle a fuller schedule than your sister can. You've always been able to."

"Count your lucky stars about it, too," my dad remarked, returning to his paper, "or we'd make you quit art lessons the way we're making her quit cheerleading."

I stared, totally shocked.

"Wait . . . you made her *quit* cheerleading?"

"The SATs are more important than cheerleading," said my dad. He would think that, seeing as how in high school, he was pretty much like . . . well, like Harold, from the stories I've heard.

"She's just taking some time off," Mom said. "If she brings her grades up, she can get back on the team. We spoke to the coach. She understands that it just got to be too much . . . cheerleading, homework . . ."

"It wouldn't have gotten to be too much," my

dad said, from behind the paper, "if a certain person didn't come down every weekend and expect to spend every waking moment with her."

"Now, Richard," Mom said. "I spoke to the Ryders. And they agreed to have a word with Jack—"

"Lot of good that will do," my dad said with a grunt, still not looking out from behind the paper. "The guy never listens to them—"

"Richard," my mother said.

I took this as my cue to leave the room. It is never fun listening to my parents fight about Lucy's boyfriend. Which they do almost every time his name comes up. Not that they aren't in complete agreement in their opinion of him: They both hate his guts. They just have different ideas over how best to handle the situation. My mom believes if they in any way try to thwart the relationship, that will only make Lucy's affection for Jack stronger—sort of like how Hellboy's affection for Liz just got stronger after they tried to keep him from seeing her when she fled to the mental institution.

My dad, on the other hand, thinks they should just forbid Lucy from seeing Jack anymore, and that will take care of the problem.

Which is why Lucy and Jack are still going out. Because everyone (except my dad) knows that telling a girl she can't go out with some guy just makes her want to go out with that guy even more.

This is another way in which Lucy's life is vastly superior to my own. She gets to date a guy my parents don't like or trust, causing them to worry about her all the time.

Lucky Lucy.

Although, if you think about it, her luck has kind of run out—at least about the cheerleading thing. I mean, it might be undermining the feminist cause, but she really loved doing it. And now it's been stripped away from her.

And yet, she hadn't looked too unhappy down there with old Harold. Which is weird, because, regardless of whether or not she misses cheerleading, one thing she's definitely going to miss, if Mom and Dad have their way, is Jack. . . . Where IS he, anyway? Why isn't he beating down the door, insisting on seeing her? Had Dr. and Mrs. Ryder had "a word" with him, as my mom had said they were going to?

But Jack, being an urban rebel and all, isn't

the type to agree not to see his girlfriend just because his parents say she's having trouble in school, and he needs to give it a rest, or whatever. In fact, since he started at RISD, Jack has been playing up the malcontent artist thing more than ever, what with the new motorcycle, and all.

And okay, my parents have expressly forbidden Lucy to ride it, even though Jack bought her a helmet (not that Lucy was particularly thrilled with it. She'd wanted a pink one. Also, she says it mashes her hair down).

But that doesn't mean Jack can't use the bike to cruise by our house, as I often hear him doing, in the middle of the night. . . .

Although, come to think of it, I hadn't actually heard the roar of Jack's Harley too often lately. What's up with that? I would have to find out from Luce after Harold leaves.

In the meantime, I had the package Lucy had said she'd left for me.

It was sitting right where Lucy had said she'd left it, in the middle of my bed. I looked inside the nondescript brown paper bag and saw two boxes. The first said, RIBBED FOR HER PLEASURE! in masculine-looking type.

Oh my God. My sister bought me a box of condoms.

Feeling a little sick, I looked at the other box. It had curly writing with flowers on it. Inside, I found a canister and a plastic, tampon-like applicator, along with an insert.

HOW TO USE CONTRACEPTIVE FOAM, the insert said.

Oh my God.

OH MY GOD.

I shoved everything back into the box, and then the boxes back into the bag, and the bag under the bed.

This was not something I was ready for. No, no, no. Not ready. SO NOT READY. So very, very not ready.

I mean, was I, Samantha Madison, really going to do this? Was I really going to have sex with my boyfriend?

I couldn't help thinking about that girl Kris had mocked earlier in the day . . . Debra, or whatever her name was. She had had sex with her boyfriend. Allegedly, anyway. What if David and I Did It, and word got out, like it had about Deb? Would people call *me* a slut behind my back?

Probably.

Although it would hardly be worse than what they *already* call me (Freak, Goth, Satan Worshiper, Punk, Psycho, etc.).

But it wouldn't just be people at school. I mean, with my uncanny ability to get my picture in magazines (mainly their Fashion Don'ts lists, but whatever), news of my sex life would probably be spread all over the tabloids. Not that I'd ever made it a point to go around telling everyone I'm a virgin or any of that. But, you know. It would be embarrassing if my grandma read about it. . . .

It was right then that Lucy came barging into my room, without knocking, of course.

"Hey," she said breathlessly, having clearly just run up the stairs. "Can I borrow your calculator?"

I glared at her. "What happened to yours?"

"I loaned it to Tiffany the last time we were at The Cheesecake Factory and were trying to figure out how much tip to leave, and she forgot to give it back. Come on, just let me borrow yours for tonight. I'll get mine back tomorrow."

I handed her my calculator. It was actually the least I could do, considering the *present* she'd left me.

"Oh, thanks," she said. And started to leave.

"Wait—" I said. *Thank you for the condoms and spermicide.* That's what I *wanted* to say. What came out instead was, "How's it going? I mean, with, um, Harold?"

"Oh," Lucy said, smoothing a silky strand of titian hair behind one ear. "Fine. You know, Harold thinks it isn't because I'm not smart that I did so poorly. He thinks I suffer from test anxiety."

"Really?"

"Yeah. Harold thinks if I apply myself, I can raise my score by a hundred points—maybe more—just by practicing some breathing exercises before I go into the examination room."

"Wow," I said, wondering if that's why Harold always seemed to need his inhaler. You know, from all the breathing exercises he must have to do to keep up his perfect GPA.

"Yeah," Lucy said. "Harold's really nice, you know. Once you get past the stuff about *Deep Space Nine* and how mad he is that they canceled *Angel*."

"Yeah," I said. "I know. I've always liked Harold. He's nice. Like when you mess something up in computer lab, he doesn't get all, *Well, did you*

114

make a back-up disk? the way some of the TAs do."

"Aw," Lucy said. "That's sweet. I can't believe he's not more popular. I mean, how come I've never met him before, like at a party or something?"

"Um," I said. "Because guys like Harold don't get invited to the kind of parties your friends throw."

"What are you talking about? My friends aren't exclusionary."

I raised my eyebrows. This was clearly an SAT word, courtesy of Harold.

"Um," I said, again. "Yeah. They kinda are."

Lucy didn't like hearing that. I could tell, since she looked right at me and went, "Well, thanks for the calculator. I better get back to Harold."

Then she left, before I even had a chance to thank her for what she had loaned me. Well, not loaned me, exactly, since I highly doubted she wanted any of it back. . . .

It was right as I was thinking this that my cell phone went off.

I so wasn't expecting it to happen—my cell phone to ring and all. I'm still not completely used to it—that I totally screamed, causing Rebecca, in her room down the hall, to call, "Do

115

you mind, Sam? I'm at a really crucial stage in this larvae dissection."

Which, actually, I would rather not have known.

I could see from the caller ID that it was David calling. David, with whom I hadn't spoken—sort of on purpose—since last night's discussion beneath the weeping willow in my front yard. I had already ignored two of his messages. I *had* to pick up.

Only . . . what was I going to say?

"Hi," seemed like a good way to start.

"Hey," David said.

Except that this was no simple "Hey." Never, in fact, had more been conveyed in such a short word in the entire history of time. All of David's happiness that I'd finally answered, as well as his frustration over not having heard back from me in over twenty-four hours, and—I really don't think I'm imagining this—even his lack of certainty about how I felt about his invitation to "play Parcheesi" with him over Thanksgiving weekend was in that *Hey*.

I'm pretty sure.

That's a lot of stuff in a single word.

"Where have you been?" David went on to

ask. Not in any sort of angry way. Just curious. "I left two messages. Are you all right?"

"Um," I said. "Yeah. Sorry. Things have just been crazy." I noticed the brown bag containing Lucy's "gifts" to me sticking out from under the bed and quickly toed it back so that the dust ruffle covered it. Don't ask me why. I mean, it wasn't like David was there in the room with me. Except that he was. Sort of. "With school, you know. And work."

"Oh," David said. "Okay. Well, what did they say?"

For one second, I honestly forgot what he was talking about. "What did who say?"

"Your parents," he said. "About Thanksgiving."

And it all came flooding back.

"Oh, Thanksgiving," I said. Oh my God. Thanksgiving. He wanted to know about Thanksgiving.

Well, of course he did. I mean, that was why I'd been dodging his calls for the past twenty-four hours. Because I knew he wanted an answer about Thanksgiving.

It was just that I wasn't sure I was ready to give him one.

"Um," I said, glancing at Manet, who as usual

was collapsed across my bed, completely oblivious to the fact that his owner's life was being turned completely upside down and inside out. Dogs have it so easy. "Yeah. Sorry. I . . . I haven't had a chance to ask them yet."

Okay. Just lied to my boyfriend. For the first time ever. More or less.

"Oh," David said.

Just like with his "Hey" a few minutes earlier, that "Oh" conveyed a lot. It actually had been less of an "Oh," than an "Oh?"

I was so dead.

"It's just," I said, suddenly speaking a mile a minute. "It's Lucy. She bombed her SATs and now my parents have made her quit cheerleading and get a tutor and everyone is freaking out."

"Whoa," David said. He sounded as if he believed me. Well, why shouldn't he? That part was the truth, anyway. "How badly did she do?"

"Really badly," I said. "So now isn't the best time to ask. If you know what I mean."

"Totally," David said. "I hear you."

The thing was, for a guy who was waiting to find out whether or not he was going to, you know, get to have sex with his girlfriend next

118

week, he sounded awfully . . . calm. I mean, not like the guys in those books of Lucy's, who are always all, *"Phillippa . . . I* must *have you. My loins burn for you."*

I was fully not getting any burning-loin vibe from David. Like, at *all*.

Which I guess I can understand. I mean, it's good he isn't getting his hopes up too much. Because it's not like, when we Do It and all, I will actually know what I'm doing, in spite of having read up on contraceptive foam usage.

Of course, he won't know what he's doing, either. Because it's not like he's any more experienced in the boudoir than I am.

But still. There's a much stronger possibility of me messing things up than him. I am not the world's most coordinated person. I barely passed P.E. (Well, to be fair, that's because I'm so noncompetitive that I refused to participate most of the time. I just didn't see the point. *Catch the ball, chase the ball, throw the ball.* Who cares? It's just a stupid ball.)

I guess I was just going to have to trust that, when—or if—the Big Moment came, my body would tell me what to do. I mean, it hadn't let me down so far.

Except for that whole rope-climbing thing in P.E.

"Well, listen," David said, still not sounding like a guy whose loins were aflame, or whatever. "Just let me know. Oh, and about tomorrow night?"

Tomorrow night? What about tomorrow night? Were we supposed to be doing something tomorrow night?

Oh, that's right. Tomorrow was Saturday. Date night. Oh my God, were we going to go out? If we went out, would he bring it up? The whole Thanksgiving plan, I mean? Tomorrow's too soon! I can't decide about all of this by tomorrow! I'm still getting used to the idea! I don't know! I don't know what I want!

"Um," I said, amazed I could sound so calm about the whole thing. "Oh, right. Tomorrow. What about it?"

"My dad's got a thing all day at the Four Seasons. It's a Return to Family thing, to garner support with some special interest groups, and so he wants me there, because . . . you know."

"Right," I said. "Family and all."

"Right. But you can totally come, if you want to."

So I can sit next to you in front of a plate of gross congealing hotel food I didn't even order myself while listening to another one of your dad's boring speeches on the off chance that we might get a chance to make out in my front yard later? Um, no thanks.

That's what I wanted to say. Instead, I said, "Gosh, that sounds fun. I think I'm busy, though. Have a good time."

David laughed. "I thought that's what you'd say. Okay."

And just like that, I was off the hook. For the whole Thanksgiving discussion.

"I know things must be weird," David said, "with Lucy and all of that. But call me, will you? I really miss you."

"I miss you, too," I said. That wasn't a lie, either. I did miss him.

"Love you, Sharona," David said.

"Love you, Daryl," I said. And hung up.

And thought, God. I am the worst girlfriend on the entire face of the planet.

Top ten ways you can tell that your boyfriend really loves you:

10. He puts up with your weird mood swings, even the one where you have PMS and you accuse him of liking Fergie of the Black-Eyed Peas better than he likes you, although you know perfectly well he's never actually met Fergie.

9. He lets you pick the movie most of the time.

8. Ditto what dessert you guys are going to share.

7. He knows your friends' names and asks how they're doing (although in David's case this isn't exactly hard, since I basically have only one friend).

6. He makes sure (to the best of his ability) that when you come over for dinner, the White House chef is serving something you will actually eat.

5. He calls, often, just to see what you're doing.

4. He thinks you look great even when you don't have any makeup on.

3. He listens when you whine about your problems and tries to offer you viable solutions for them, even if most of the things he suggests are totally stupid and would never work because he's a guy and he just doesn't understand.

2. He doesn't get upset when he overhears you going on with your best friend about how hot you think that new guy on *Gilmore Girls* is.

And the number-one way you can tell that your boyfriend really loves you:

1. He doesn't make a big deal out of it when you opt to spend your Saturday night in front of the TV instead of with him.

6

$\mathcal{E}xcept$ that I didn't get to. Spend Saturday night watching *National Geographic Explorer* with Rebecca, I mean. Because at around three o'clock, the phone rang, and when I picked it up, I was surprised to hear Dauntra on the other end.

"Sam?" For some reason, she was yelling. I soon realized why. Wherever she was, it was *really* noisy in the background.

"Dauntra?" I was kind of surprised to hear from her. Dauntra had never called my house before. I didn't even know she had my number. I mean, all of the Potomac Video employees' phone numbers are posted on the bulletin board in Stan's office, but I didn't know Dauntra had copied mine down. "What's all that noise? Where *are* you?"

"Some police station," Dauntra yelled. I heard someone in the background going, "Put that down, or the cuffs are going back on."

"A *police* station?" I echoed. "What are you doing in a police station? Are you all right?"

"I'm fine," Dauntra said cheerfully. "I'm just under arrest."

"Arrest?" I nearly dropped the phone. "You mean . . . you're calling me from JAIL?"

"Uh-huh," Dauntra said. "Because I don't think I'm going to be out in time to make my shift at the store tonight. Can you do it for me? Four to closing? I promise I'll make it up to you someday!"

I was still in shock over where she was. Also, I was glad neither of my parents or Theresa was around to overhear my end of the conversation. I wasn't sure how excited they'd be over someone from work calling me from jail.

"What did you get arrested for?" I asked her.

"What?" Dauntra moved the phone away from her mouth and yelled, "You guys, SHUT UP, I can't hear her." Then she said, into the receiver, "What'd you say, Sam?"

"I said, What did you get arrested for?"

"Oh, that," Dauntra said. "A bunch of us did

a die-in. In front of the Four Seasons, you know, where your buddy the president is having his big fund-raiser. Boy, was he ever surprised!"

Um, he wasn't the only one. I couldn't believe what I was hearing, either.

"So, can you take my shift or not?" Dauntra wanted to know. "And if you can't, can you call around and see if anybody else can? I only get one phone call, and I really don't want to lose my job."

"You only get one phone call, and you called me?" I was shocked. "Dauntra, shouldn't you call a lawyer?" Then I remembered something. "My mom's a lawyer. Tell me where you are, and I'll get her to go down there and—"

"I don't need a lawyer," Dauntra said. "Somebody'll be posting my bail soon. But not in time for me to make my shift. So will you do it?"

"Sure," I said. "I mean, of course. I mean—" I heard someone on Dauntra's end of the line shout an obscenity. "Oh my God, Dauntra. Be careful!"

"Careful?" Dauntra laughed. "I'm having a blast! Thanks, Sam!"

And then she hung up.

Which was how I found myself, an hour later,

manning the cash register at Potomac Video and trying to find a channel on one of the shop's overhead TVs that was showing the demonstration where Dauntra got herself arrested.

Sadly, the TVs at Potomac Video aren't hooked up to cable, since they're just supposed to be used to show whatever movie we're trying to promote that week. So all I could get was snow. Finally, Stan made me quit and put in the latest Jason Bourne DVD. He hadn't seemed too surprised when I showed up for Dauntra's shift.

"I don't even want to know," he said, when I attempted to feed him my (made-up) excuse for where Dauntra was (visiting a sick aunt). "Just watch out for shoplifters. We get a ton of them Saturday nights. Stupid neighborhood kids with nothing else to do. They think it's hilarious to rip off an Xbox game or two."

I was at the cash register watching for stupid neighborhood kids when the overhead bell on the front door to the store tinkled. But instead of Mr. Wade or one of the other regulars coming in to complain about our lack of selection, my sister Lucy walked in.

This was a huge surprise, because so far as I knew, Lucy hadn't set foot inside Potomac

Video for years. Popular people like Lucy don't have time to watch DVDs, as they are much too busy going to parties and making out with their boyfriends. True, Lucy did spend the occasional Friday night at home, but she always let the video-choosing be done by someone else. Potomac Video, with its life-size cardboard cutouts of Boba Fett and Han Solo, open duct work in the ceiling, and hand-printed signs (RESTROOM FOR EMPLOYEES ONLY. EVERYONE ELSE JUST HAS TO HOLD IT), was hardly Lucy's kind of place.

You could totally see that she was thinking as much herself as she made her way past the New Releases shelf—attracting the admiration of just about everyone in the place, most of whom were college-age guys in Kiss the Geek T-shirts, arguing over which *Star Trek* movie to rent. When she finally saw me at the register, her face crumpled in relief, and she came hurrying up to the counter—oblivious of the jaws she caused to slacken along her way—and went, "Hey, Sam."

"Um," I said. "Hey. What are you doing here?" Because I would have thought she'd have been out with Jack, or some of her girlfriends, at the very least.

Then I remembered.

"God," I said, horrified on her behalf. "Did they ground you, too?"

Lucy looked confused. "Who?"

"Mom and Dad," I said. "You know. For the SAT thing."

She went, with a laugh, "No, they didn't ground me."

I stared down at her. On the TVs all around us, Matt Damon's image flickered as he said, "They killed the woman that I love!" The geeks over in Sci-Fi, I noticed, were staring at Lucy with the exact same look of intense longing that Matt wore.

"Well, then," I said, a little confused myself, "what are you doing *here*?"

"Oh." Lucy shifted her tiny little Louis Vuitton bag (a gift for her birthday from Grandma) from one shoulder to the other. "I thought I might rent a DVD. You might have heard of it. Something called *Hellboy*?"

I stared at her. "*Hellboy*," I said.

"Yeah." Lucy looked around the store. As soon as her head moved in the direction of the geeks over in Sci-Fi, they ducked, and pretended to be engrossed in the cover of the new *Alien* movie.

"Do you guys have it?"

"*Hellboy*," I repeated. "With Ron Perlman and Selma Blair. Made in 2004. Based on the Dark Horse comic of the same name. THAT *Hellboy*?"

"I guess so," Lucy said, looking blank. "I don't know. Harold recommended it."

I stared at her even harder. "Harold MINSKY?"

"Yes," she said. "He said it's one of his favorite movies of all time. I thought I heard you talking about it, too. Didn't you like it? I thought so." She'd reached out to touch one of the *Nightmare Before Christmas* action figures Dauntra had wrapped around the *Need a Penny? Take a Penny. Have a Penny? Give a Penny* tray. "So. Do you have it?"

Without taking my eyes off my sister, I said, to the geeks in Sci-Fi, "Hey. One of you grab *Hellboy* and throw it over here."

A second later, a copy of *Hellboy* landed in my hands.

Lucy glanced over at the geeks and smiled. "Oh, *thank* you," she said.

The geeks, mortified, scattered for the safety of Documentaries.

"Here you go," I said, and handed Lucy the DVD.

She looked at the cover and said, "Oh. My. So

130

that's Hellboy, there, with the bumpy things on his head?"

"They're horns," I said. "He files them down."

"Oh," Lucy said. "Is he, um, nice? Because he looks . . . not nice."

"That," I said, "is the conflict. Hellboy is a demon constantly at odds with his own nature. He is Satan on Earth, yet was raised with loving care by people who had the good of mankind at heart, and now, as an adult, Hellboy has pledged to fight his own nature and save the world from evil. He is redeemed by his love for Liz, who is at odds with her own genetic destiny as a fire-starter."

"Oh," Lucy said. "That's nice. Okay, well, I'll take it. How much do I owe you?"

"A buck," I said. "I'll give you my employee discount, since you're family."

"Great," Lucy said, and dug around in her purse. As she did so, she asked casually, keeping her gaze on the gum-blackened floor, "You know Harold, right, Sam? I mean, socially?"

I blinked at her. This wasn't exactly flattering, considering the social circles in which Harold travels. Also . . . where was this sudden fascination with Harold Minsky coming from?

"Um," I said. "Not exactly. I mean, he's my computer lab TA. But we don't exactly have the same friends. I'm a nerd. But not *that* big of a nerd."

"Yeah, but you collect comic books like he does, and stuff," Lucy said.

"Manga," I corrected her. "Harold collects manga. I like to draw it."

"Whatever." Lucy found her dollar and handed it over. "The point is—have you ever heard about him having a girlfriend?"

I was so shocked, I nearly fell over.

"HAROLD? HAROLD MINSKY?" What girl would *touch* him? I mean, with that hair? "No. Harold doesn't have a girlfriend."

"I didn't think so," Lucy said, looking thoughtful. "That's what makes it so weird."

"What makes what so weird?"

"Well, the fact that he doesn't seem to like me," she said. "I mean, he likes me, I guess. But he doesn't seem to *like* me. What I mean is—"

"I know what you mean," I cut her off. "You mean he hasn't hit on you."

"Well, yeah," Lucy said. "It's just so . . . weird."

The thing is, you can't even get mad at her, really, for saying something like that. She genuinely doesn't know any better. Lucy is the kind of girl guys *always* hit on—all guys, except ones who are gay, or taken, like David. Having a guy not hit on her, the way Harold apparently hadn't, was a whole new experience for her.

And evidently, not one she particularly relished (SAT word meaning "to appreciate or enjoy").

"Lucy," I said. "Mom and Dad like Harold because they think he's the type of boy who *won't* hit on you. So unless you want someone even worse"—although to tell the truth, there really isn't anyone worse than Harold, nerdiness-wise. Except maybe someone from Rebecca and David's school—"I wouldn't complain, if I were you."

"I'm not going to complain," Lucy said, giving me a look that clearly said, "Are you crazy?" "It's just *weird*, is all. I mean, *all* boys like me. Why doesn't he?"

Now I felt a burst of irritation with her. True, Lucy can be the coolest of sisters—case in point, the contraceptive foam she'd gotten me.

But she's also one of the vainest people on the planet.

"Not everybody judges people on how they

look, Luce," I said to her. "I mean, I'm sure in your circle of friends, that's *de rigueur*"—(SAT word meaning "conventional or fitting")—"but Harold has probably learned to judge people more on their insides than their outsides."

When Lucy just looked at me blankly, I tapped the cover of the DVD she was renting.

"Like *him*," I said, pointing at Hellboy. "He looks evil, right? But he's not. You can't always judge people by how they look. Ugly people might be beautiful inside. And beautiful people might be ugly inside. That's all I'm saying. Maybe Harold thinks your insides leave something to be desired."

"Why?" Lucy demanded tartly. "I'm not *evil*. Or stupid, either, if that's what you're thinking. Just because I don't know what waggish means is no reason—"

"Why do you even care, anyway?" I asked her—just to make sure, you know, that she wasn't, against all laws of nature, falling for Harold. "Don't you already have a boyfriend? Where *is* Jack, anyway?"

"Oh," Lucy said, keeping her gaze on the floor again. "He didn't come down this weekend. I told him not to. You know, on account of how

Mom and Dad are so upset about this SAT thing."

"Yeah," I said, a little more sympathetically. "I heard about Bare Essentials. And cheerleading. That must suck."

"Whatever," Lucy said with a shrug. "I was kind of over cheerleading, anyway. It isn't as much fun when you're the one in charge. I mean, now that I'm a senior, I'm supposed to help make up the routines and stuff. It's way too much responsibility. Know what I mean?"

I wasn't sure I'd ever heard anyone refer to making up a cheerleading routine as too difficult of a responsibility. But I figured I had to take her word for it. I mean, God knew I had never made up a routine. Maybe it *was* hard. As hard as integrating the subject of a drawing with its background. Who knew?

"Was Jack mad?" I asked her. "I mean, how did he take it?" Because Jack is the sort of person who expects to be treated like he's the most important thing in everyone's life.

"Oh, he had a cow," Lucy said cheerfully. "He wanted to know why he couldn't be my tutor . . . like *his* scores were that much better than mine. Mom and Dad put the kibosh on that right away. They were all, *How much studying will you two do, anyway?* Plus Dr. and Mrs. Ryder want him to concentrate on his own school stuff. He hasn't really been paying much attention to it, coming down here every weekend, and all of that. He got an F on some project, and they were all bent out of shape about it."

I could easily imagine this. The Ryders had to pull a lot of strings to get Jack into RISD in the first place, on account of his below-average grades. I guess his whole theory on how grades don't prove anything didn't really work out the way he'd planned.

"So I guess you're really gonna miss him," I said, trying to offer some sisterly solace. "Jack, I mean. While you two are apart, getting your grades and stuff back up."

"I guess so," Lucy said, a little vaguely. "Do you think Harold likes chocolate chip cookies? Because I was thinking I might make him some. As a sort of thank you, for tutoring me."

"Mom and Dad are *paying* him to tutor you," I pointed out. "You don't have to make him cookies."

"I know," Lucy said. "But it never hurts to be nice to people." She picked up the bag with the DVD in it. "Well, thanks."

"You're welcome." Then, realizing maybe I was being ridiculous—I mean, LUCY? Falling for Harold Minsky? Please—I added, "And, uh, thank you, too. For the, um. You know. Package you left me."

"Oh, no problem," Lucy said, with a twinkle that caused one of the geeks to bump into the life-size Boba Fett cutout, then hasten to right it.

"Hey, Madison." Stan suddenly appeared at my side, and stood blinking down at Lucy. "This a friend of yours?"

"My sister," I said. "Lucy. Lucy, this is the night manager, Stan."

"How do you do," Lucy said politely, while Stan just stared down at Lucy as if she had stepped off the front of an *Amazing Nurse Nanako* video.

"Hi," he breathed. Then, getting a hold of himself, he said, "Listen, Madison, you want to head home with your sister, go ahead. I'll close up."

I looked at the clock on the wall. There were fifteen whole minutes until my shift was up. And he was letting me go home early! God, it was great sometimes, having such a hot sister.

"Thanks, Stan," I said, and grabbed my coat and backpack.

"Uh, wait a sec," Stan said, as I started to slip beneath the counter to join Lucy.

Then I remembered and silently handed him my backpack, which he opened and quickly flicked through, while Lucy looked on, curious.

"There ya go," Stan said when he was through, handing my bag back to me. "Have a nice night."

"Thanks," I said. "See ya."

And Lucy and I walked out together into the crisp night air.

"Does he search *everybody's* backpack before they leave," Lucy wanted to know, as soon as the door had shut behind us, "or just yours?"

"Everyone's," I said.

"God," Lucy said. "Doesn't that make you mad?"

"I don't know," I said. The truth was, I had way bigger things to worry about than whether or not my bag got searched after work. I would have thought Lucy did, too. "Didn't they search your bag at Bare Essentials?"

"No."

"Well," I said thoughtfully, "you can't really make as much selling bras on eBay as you can selling stolen DVDs."

"What, are you kidding?" Lucy snorted.

"Some of those bras retail for as much as eighty bucks. I'm really surprised at you, Sam, putting up with that kind of treatment. From that Stan guy, I mean. It's not like you."

"Well, what am I supposed to do about it?" I grumbled. "Have a die-in?"

"I don't know," Lucy said. "But *something*."

Which was all well and good for her to say. I mean, Mom and Dad weren't making *her* work anymore. I needed my job. If I wanted to pay for my art supplies, I mean.

I should have known, then. I mean, her showing up at Potomac Video like that should have been my first warning sign as to what was going on with Lucy.

But I was too involved in my own problems to pay attention to hers. Especially considering the fact that my problems? They were about to get a whole lot bigger.

Top ten ways I suck as a girlfriend:

10. Instead of going out with my boyfriend on Saturday night, I choose to fill in at work for someone who was arrested that day for protesting something my boyfriend's father feels very strongly about.

9. Then I don't call him.

8. My boyfriend, I mean. Even though he asked me to. Even after I get home from work that night, and I see on the news that hundreds of people were arrested for pretending to die in front of the very hotel he was having dinner in.

7. And when he (my boyfriend) calls, I let it go to

voice mail. Because I just can't deal.

6. Even though I know he's probably hurting.

5. Because those people look as if they really, really hate his dad.

4. But I have too many problems of my own. Like, for instance, I need to decide if I agree with him. My boyfriend, I mean. About us being ready. For you-know-what.

3. I'm not sure I do.

2. At least, not most of the time.

And the number-one reason I suck as a girl-friend:

1. I don't call him the next day, either. Or pick up the phone when he calls me.

7

"*They* were just all so . . . dirty." That is what Catherine has to say about the protesters. The ones she saw on the news. The same ones who were outside the Four Seasons when Dauntra got arrested. The ones Dauntra was arrested with. "I mean, like they hadn't bathed in weeks."

"They were having a die-in," I pointed out. "Pretending to be dead. So they were lying on the street. That's why they looked dirty."

"It wasn't just street dirt," Catherine said firmly, as she searched through the apples at the fruit and salad bar in the caf for one that wasn't bruised into pulp. "They just looked . . . homeless. I mean, couldn't they have worn nicer clothes?"

"They aren't going to wear their Sunday best to lie in the street, Cath," I said.

"Yeah, but I'm just saying. If they want people to be more sympathetic to their cause, you'd think they'd at least take out some of their piercings, or whatever. I mean, how are we supposed to relate to people like that? It's bad enough they were totally dissing the president. Did they have to look so . . . grungy?"

"They weren't dissing the president," I said. "They were protesting his policies—"

Before I had time to go on, however, Kris Parks came bustling up to us, and was all, "What are you guys doing here? You said you'd help set up the gym!"

I had absolutely no idea what she was talking about. It was Catherine who elbowed me and went, "For the town hall meeting tomorrow. Remember?"

"Oh, right," I said, trying not to sound as bummed as I felt. Because the last thing I wanted to do was spend my lunch hour setting up folding chairs with Kris Parks and her hideous Right Wayers.

"Come ON," Kris said, grabbing my arm. "I told everyone you'd show."

Everyone turned out to be . . . well, everyone. Not just the Right Wayers and other people from Adams Prep, either, including my German teacher, Frau Rider, who kept wandering around, shouting, "Don't spill that paint on the gym floor!"

No, Kris had also invited members of the press. To watch me, the girl who saved the president, set up folding chairs.

Not that many had actually shown up. Fortunately, most papers prefer to run stories that include real news, not stuff about some prep school's efforts to get ready for a presidential visitation. Or maybe they'd caught on that the whole thing had just been a ploy on Kris's part to get herself into the papers, and therefore add another clipping to her college admissions packets.

But a few of the free press papers had shown up, and their photographers busily snapped away as I was painting a huge sign that said, WELCOME TO ADAMS PREP, MR. PRESIDENT, bored out of my skull.

At least until Debra Mullins, the dance team member about whom Kris had been so mean the week before, wandered by, and asked, in her bright, chipper voice, "What are you guys doing?"

Kris, ever conscious of the cameras on her,

went, "Setting up for the president's visit here on Tuesday night."

"The president is coming *here*?" Debra looked impressed. "To Adams Prep?"

"Yes," Kris replied. "Maybe if you spent less time under the bleachers with your boyfriend, and more time paying attention in class, you might have realized this."

Debra blinked a few times at this. To tell you the truth, so did I.

"Was that really necessary?" I asked Kris, after Debra had wandered confusedly away.

Kris looked at me blankly. She had no idea what I was talking about. "Was what really necessary?" she asked.

"That," I said, jabbing the end of my paint brush in Debra's direction. "What you said to her."

Kris smirked. "I don't see why not," she said. "It's the truth, isn't it?"

"Yeah, but he's her boyfriend. If she wants to hang out with him under the bleachers, what business of that is yours?"

"I'd hardly call what Deb and Jeff do together *hanging out*, Sam. *Hooking up* is more like it."

It was only when I saw Kris's eyes narrow that

I realized what was going on. And that's that all of the reporters who'd been milling around in a bored sort of way, cursing their editors for giving them such a sucky assignment, suddenly perked up and started paying attention to what we were saying. *This was good*, you could practically hear them thinking. The Girl Who Saved the President Picking a Fight With the Head of Right Way? Major human interest.

"And, by the way, Sam," Kris said, forcing a smile. Because she obviously couldn't say what she wanted to say. Which was *Get bent, Sam.* "I didn't know you and Deb were such good friends."

"We're not friends," I snapped.

Then felt guilty. Because that had made it sound as if I wouldn't be friends with a girl like Deb on account of her being a "slut," when the reality was, I wouldn't be friends with a girl like Deb because she's on the dance team, and I can't stand people with school spirit. I mean, the dance team performs at halftime during the football games and stuff.

"What I mean is—"

But I never got to say what I meant, because at that moment, my cell phone rang.

David. It had to be David.

146

And I still wasn't ready to talk to David.

Everyone was looking at me. Kris. Catherine. Frau "Don't Spill Paint on the Gym Floor" Rider. The reporters.

My cell phone rang again. "Harajuku Girls." That's the ring I'd chosen, from the Gwen Stefani song.

"Well," Kris said, "aren't you going to answer it?"

Frustrated, I pulled the phone from my jeans pocket. I was going to turn off the ringer, but before I could, Kris got a glimpse of the caller ID screen as it flashed David's name.

"Oooooh," she said, in a loud voice. "It's the first son!"

Now every television camera in the place was on, and the lens pointed straight at me.

I couldn't ignore David's call. Not this time.

Feeling sick to my stomach, I answered. "Hello?"

"Sam?" Again, David managed to convey a thousand different emotions in a single word— relief that I'd finally answered, happiness at hearing my voice, confusion and frustration over my having given him the cold shoulder for the past two days . . . maybe even a little anger about it, too.

"There you are. Where have you been? I've been trying to reach you since Saturday night."

"Yeah," I said, conscious of the cameras on me. "I know. Sorry, things have been crazy. How are you?"

"You think they've been crazy for *you*?" David asked, laughing. "Have you turned on a TV lately? Did you see what happened Saturday night? Too bad you didn't go. You'd have loved it."

"Yeah," I said. "Probably. Actually, David, now is not a very good time to talk."

"Well, when *would* be a good time to talk, Sam?" David asked. He didn't sound like he was laughing anymore. "You've barely spoken to me since Thursday. I mean, do you have *any* openings for me in your busy schedule?"

"Hey," I said. "YOU'RE the one who went out with your *parents* on Saturday." Which, even as I said it, I realized wasn't fair. I mean, he *had* invited me to come along.

And it isn't as if his parents are just . . . well, like *normal* parents.

"What's wrong, Sam?" David, sounding confused, wanted to know. "And don't tell me nothing. I know something's up. Are you mad at me, or something?"

Suddenly I became aware of how quiet it had grown in the gym. Which was weird because there were a lot of people in it, all busy doing fairly loud things, like opening folding chairs and arranging them in long rows.

But none of that was going on right now. Instead, everyone in the gym was simply standing where they were, looking at me. Even Catherine had her paint brush poised in midair ("Don't spill paint on the gym floor!" Frau Rider hissed) as she stared at me. The only sound you could hear was the whir of the television cameras, as they filmed me.

"Because it seems like," David's voice went on in my ear, starting to sound less confused, and more angry, "that ever since I asked you about Thanksgiving, you've been mad at me. And I want to know why. I mean, what did I do?"

"Nothing," I said, staring daggers at Kris Parks, who had a little cat-who-swallowed-the-canary grin on her face. All because I'd been caught on film, arguing with my boyfriend. "I have to go now. I'll explain why later."

"You mean you'll explain why you have to go now later?" David wanted to know. "Or why you're so mad at me?"

149

"I'm not," I said. "Really. I'll explain later."

"Really? Or will you be dodging my calls again later?"

"Really," I said. Then added, desperately hoping he'd understand something I didn't even understand myself, "Love you."

"Love you, too," he said. Only in a sort of impatient way. Then he hung up.

I hung up, too. Then put my phone away. Then, cheeks blazing, and eyes on my feet, went back to the sign I'd been painting.

"Everything all right?" Catherine asked gently, handing me the paint brush I'd abandoned.

"Fine," I said, trying to put some artistic flair into the letters I was filling in—the ENT in PRESIDENT.

"That's good to know," Kris Parks said, as she bent over her letters—SID. "I'd hate for there to be trouble in paradise."

Which was when, for reasons I will never understand, I kicked the paint can, so it went rolling all over the banner reading WELCOME TO ADAMS PREP, MR. PRESIDENT. All over the shoes of the people working on the sign. And all over the gym floor.

"Aaiiiii!" screamed Frau Rider, when she saw this.

"Sam!" cried Catherine, leaping out of the way.

"You bitch!" shouted Kris Parks, when she saw what I'd done to her Kenneth Coles.

Which was when I dropped my paint brush in the middle of the free throw line and walked away.

Top ten ways to keep yourself occupied during after-school detention at John Adams Preparatory Academy:

10. Finish Trig homework.

9. Bite nails.

8. Attempt to do assigned German reading.

7. Wonder what your parents are going to do when they find out you got detention.

6. Decide they probably will forbid you from going to Camp David with your boyfriend for Thanksgiving.

5. Decide this probably wouldn't be such a bad thing.

4. Write personal essay due in English class, *What Patriotism Means to Me.* Write that patriotism means disagreeing with the government without having to go to jail.

3. Make your own manga. Only not one of those lame ones with boys who turn into cuddly rabbits or whatever when the heroine hugs them. But a cool one, where the heroine is on a mission to avenge her family, like Uma Thurman in *Kill Bill*, and kills everyone who stands in her way.

2. Give up on manga after five frames because it is too hard and try to draw your boyfriend from memory instead, concentrating on the whole and not the parts.

And the number-one thing to do in detention at Adams Prep:

1. Wonder if your boyfriend even likes you anymore, after the way you've been treating him. And worry that he may come to his senses and realize he could easily get a girlfriend who is much less of a head case than you.

8

My parents were uncharacteristically cool about the detention thing. As soon as they heard Kris Parks had been involved, they were just like, "Oh. Well, don't do it again."

Even Theresa went, "I'm proud of you, Sam, for not dumping the paint over her head."

Which made me realize I really have made a lot of progress this year, growing as a human being. Because last year, I definitely would have done that. Dumped the paint over Kris's head, not her shoes.

Nobody bothered to ask *why* I'd done it. Accidentally on purpose kick paint all over the gym floor, I mean. Nobody except Lucy, I mean, who came fluttering into my room after dinner, while I was scowling at my German assignment.

"So," she said, flopping down next to Manet

on my bed, without waiting to be invited to do so. "What's up with you and David?"

"Nothing," I said, feeling a spurt of annoyance toward her. Don't even ask me why. I mean, she'd been nothing but nice to me, what with the condom/foam thing, and all.

Probably it wasn't Lucy I was annoyed with. Probably, *I* was the one I was annoyed with. Because I still hadn't called David back. I just . . .

I just had no idea what to say to him.

"Well," Lucy said, rolling over and staring at my ceiling, "then why are you avoiding his calls?"

I stared at her. "Who says I'm avoiding his calls?"

"It's only all over school," Lucy said, in a bored voice. "Wasn't that why you got so mad and spilled the paint? Because Kris commented on it?"

"No," I lied.

"Oh," Lucy said with a little laugh. "Okay. Whatever."

But she didn't leave. She just lay there, playing with the fringe of hair over Manet's eyes. I knew she'd try to braid it or, worse, put it in tiny butterfly barrettes. I hate when she does that. Sheepdogs have hair in their face for a reason.

Their eyes are very sensitive to light.

I looked at Lucy as she finger-combed Manet's bangs into a fauxhawk. The thing is, Lucy *does* have some experience in the boy arena. There was a chance—just a slight one, but a chance all the same—that she might know how to help. After all, she'd been in my same shoes, once.

I swung my German book closed.

"It's just," I said, sitting up, "I don't know. I mean, I want to Do It with him, and all. But what if . . ."

Lucy let go of Manet's fur and shifted so that she was propping her head up on Manet's side. Manet didn't appear to notice. "What if . . . what?"

"What if, like . . . I don't like it?"

"Well, have you been practicing?" Lucy asked.

I stared down at her. "Practicing? Practicing *what*?"

"Making love," Lucy said. "Look, it's easy. Get in the bathtub. Turn the water on. Scoot down to the end of the tub, until your you-know-what is under the running water. Then pretend the water is the guy, and let it—"

"OH MY GOD."

Lucy blinked up at me. "What?" She looked totally surprised that I should be so shocked. "You haven't tried it? Dude, it totally works."

"LUCY!" I practically screamed. Loud enough, anyway, that Manet lifted his head and looked around sleepily.

"What?" Lucy asked, again. "There's nothing wrong with it."

"THAT is why you're always in the bathtub so long?" I croaked.

"Sure," Lucy said. "What'd you think I was doing in there?"

"Not THAT," I said. "I thought you were . . . I don't know. BATHING. And reading those romance novels of yours."

"Well, that, too," Lucy said. "They totally help, you know. Some of them are really descriptive. Although thinking about Orlando Bloom is supposed to help, too. While you're letting the water do its work. Orlando doesn't do it for me. But I hear he works for a lot of other girls."

I couldn't stop staring at her. "THIS is what you guys talk about at the popular table in the lunch room? Who you think about while you're—under the faucet?"

"Not at the lunch table, silly," Lucy said with

157

a laugh. "I mean, there are *guys* there. Guys don't want to hear that you think about anything but them. Believe me. But when there aren't guys around, yeah, we talk about this kind of stuff. I think Tiffany Shore was the first one to figure it out. She read about it in *Cosmo*. She uses a hand-held shower nozzle instead, though."

"OH MY GOD!" I yelled, again.

Lucy looked surprised at my outburst. "Well," she said, "girls aren't like guys. We aren't born knowing how to Do It. And you can't leave it up to the *guy*. Most of them couldn't care less about whether or not YOU get anything out of it. It's really every girl for herself out there. That's why practice is so important. Also, getting into the right mindset. That's why I usually think about that guy from *The Count of Monte Cristo*—"

"Jim Caviezel?" I interrupted, more horrified than ever.

"Yeah. He's so hot."

I could not believe I was even having this conversation.

My incredulity must have shown on my face, since Lucy added, "Come on, Sam. You can't expect a guy to know what to do to make you have an orgasm. You have to do it yourself. At least until you can teach him how."

This was all news to me.

"Did you teach Jack?" I wanted to know. Because I couldn't believe Jack had ever let anyone teach him anything. Even Lucy. I mean, he basically thinks he knows it all.

"Jack?" Lucy got a funny look on her face all of a sudden. Funny like she was going to cry.

Really. Just like that. Just from hearing his name.

And then, next thing I knew, she'd buried her face in Manet's thick gray and white fur.

"Lucy?" Alarmed, I reached out and touched her shoulder. "Are you okay? Are you . . . are you sick, or something?"

"Yes, I'm sick," Lucy said, into Manet's hip-bone. "Sick of that *name*."

I blinked down at her. Name? What name? *Jack*'s name?

"Did something happen?" I asked her worriedly. "Between you and Jack?"

Even as the words were coming out of my mouth, I realized how stupid they sounded. *Obviously* something had happened between her and Jack. Had he found some other girl, some *college* girl?

Of course not. Jack was besotted with Lucy. He would never cheat on her! So what was wrong?

I gasped, remembering what Dad had said in the living room the other night. What if Mom had finally let Dad have his way, and he'd forbidden Lucy from seeing Jack? And what if Lucy was planning on running away with him, tonight, on the back of his motorcycle, like Daryl Hannah and Aidan Quinn in that movie *Reckless* I saw on the Romance Channel? Oh my God, Lucy's even a cheerleader, like that character Daryl played! And Jack has a leather jacket, just like the guy Aidan played!

But where are they going to live if they run off together? They have no money. Lucy doesn't even have her job at Bare Essentials anymore! They'll have to live—

IN A TRAILER PARK.

LIKE DARYL AND SHARONA.

"Lucy," I said, tightening my grip on her shoulder, "you can't run off with Jack. You can't live in a trailer park. They get hit by tornadoes all the time."

Lucy lifted her face from Manet's fur and squinted at me through tear-swollen eyes. "Run off with Jack? I'm not going to run off with Jack. I'm not even going out with him anymore. I Instant Messaged him last week that we were over."

My mouth fell open. "WHAT?"

"You heard me." Lucy finally sat up, and I saw the gleaming tracks her tears had made down her cheeks. Not so amazingly, she still looked pretty, even with random strands of dog hair stuck to the tear tracks on her face.

There really is no justice in the world.

"You broke up with Jack?" I felt as if my brain were melting. "Through Instant Messaging?"

"Yeah," Lucy said, picking fur from her face. "So what?"

"Well, I mean, isn't that . . ." How could she not know this? "Isn't that kind of . . . cold?"

"I don't care," Lucy said with a sniffle. "I couldn't take his pathetic whining a second longer. He was *suffocating* me. I mean, he's in *college*. You think he'd get a life, instead of wanting to come back here all the time and *bug* me."

"Um," I said. "Well, Jack really loves you, you know. He can't help missing you."

"Yeah, but he could help being a controlling freak, couldn't he? God, it's good to have him

161

off my back. *'I can't believe you're going to the game instead of spending time with me,'* she said, in a surprisingly dead-on imitation of her former boyfriend. " *'Sometimes I think you care more about your stupid squad than you do for me.'* Like my wanting to have fun with my friends was some kind of personal insult to him!"

I couldn't believe this. Lucy and Jack, broken up? Really broken up, from the way it sounded, not just one of their many fights. Could it really be over between the two of them? That was *it*?

"But you went out with him for years and years," I said. "You guys were voted couple most likely to get *married*."

"Yeah," Lucy said. "Well, it didn't work out, did it?"

"But he was your first," I exclaimed.

"My first what?" Lucy asked.

"Hello," I said. "Your first LOVE."

Lucy made a face. "Tell me about it. If I'd known better, I wouldn't have picked anybody so moody. And so needy. If I'd have known better, I'd have picked someone more like—"

I stared at her. "Like who?"

"No one," Lucy said quickly. "Never mind."

"No, I mean it," I said. "Who? You can tell me,

Luce. I want to know. And I won't tell."

David, I thought. She's going to say David. Of course she wants a boyfriend like David. David made up white-trash names for us. She and Jack never had white-trash names for each other.

And she knows when David calls me, it's never to make sure I'm not out with some other guy, but because he genuinely cares about how I'm doing, and wants to hear how my day went.

And she sees how David walks me to the door every time he brings me home. And okay, this is also sometimes the only opportunity we have to make out, which might contribute a little to David's motivation.

But whatever. Lucy doesn't have to know that. Jack *never* walked Lucy to the door.

She wants a boyfriend more like mine. She has to.

And I can't say that I blame her. God. Now that I think about it, David is like the perfect boyfriend.

So why am I being so mean to him?

"It's just," Lucy said, with a sudden, hiccupy sob. "It's just that . . . he's so smart!"

Poor Lucy. David certainly is much smarter than Jack. There's no denying that. It's true

Jack's a gifted artist, but that doesn't necessarily make him smart. I remember he once insisted Picasso invented fauvism. Seriously.

"Yes," I said sympathetically. "Yes, he is, isn't he?"

"I mean, there's something very attractive about a guy who knows . . . well, *everything*," Lucy went on, starting to sound close to tears again. "Jack just THINKS he knows everything."

"Yes," I said, thinking Poor Lucy. If only David had a brother. "Yes, he did, didn't he?"

"I mean, all that time he was going on about being an urban rebel . . . how much of a rebel can you be if your parents are paying for everything?"

"True," I said. "Very true."

"The thing is, Jack was just a poser," Lucy said, still teary-eyed.

"Yes," I said. You could never call David a poser. He is always, solidly, exactly who he is, and no one else. "He *was* a bit of one, wasn't he?"

"I don't want to go out with a poser," Lucy said. "I want the *real* thing. I want a *real* man."

Like David. Well, you could hardly blame her.

"You'll find him," I assured her. "Someday."

"I already have," Lucy said. "Found him."

Causing me to go, "Wait. What?"

"I found him," she said with a sob. "B-but he doesn't want me!"

Then she buried her head, with a wail, into my lap.

"Wait." I looked down uncomprehendingly at the red-gold puddle of silk spread out across my thighs. "You found him? WHERE?"

"At s-school," Lucy wept.

And, even though I'd *known*, deep down, that she wasn't talking about David, this was still something of a relief. That it wasn't my boyfriend she was pining for.

"Well, that's great, Luce," I said, still feeling confused. "I mean, that you found someone so soon—"

"Aren't you even listening to me?" Lucy demanded, sitting up and glaring at me with red-rimmed eyes. "I said, he d-doesn't want me!"

"He doesn't?" I stared at her. "But why? Does he already have a girlfriend?"

"No," Lucy said, shaking her head. "Not that I know of."

"Well, is he . . . I mean, is he *gay*?" Because that was the only reason I could think of for a guy not liking my sister, if he wasn't already in love with some other girl, like David.

"No," she said. "I don't think so."

"Well, then, why—"

"I don't KNOW why," Lucy said. "I TOLD you that. I've done EVERYTHING I could to make him notice me. I wore my shortest mini last time I saw him—the one Theresa threatened to put in the trash if I wore it outside the house ever again? I spent two hours on my makeup. I even wore lip liner. And what did I get for it?" She pounded a perfectly manicured fist against the mattress. "NOTHING. He *still* doesn't know I'm alive. I asked him, you know, if he wanted to go to the movies this weekend—to the new Adam Sandler—and he said . . . he said . . . he said he HAD OTHER PLANS!"

She grabbed a pillow and clutched it to her face as she wailed into it.

"Well," I said, blinking uncomprehendingly, "maybe he did. Have other plans, I mean."

"He didn't," Lucy sobbed. "I could tell he didn't."

"Well . . . maybe he doesn't like Adam Sandler. Lots of people don't."

"That's not it," Lucy said. "It's me. He just doesn't like ME."

"Lucy," I said, "everybody likes you. Okay?

Every guy who isn't taken or likes guys and not girls likes you. It has to be something else. Who *is* this guy, anyway?"

But Lucy just shook her head and wailed, "What does it matter? What does any of it matter when he doesn't even know I'm alive?"

Lucy flopped back across the bed, weeping stormily. I stared down at her prone figure, trying to make sense of what I'd just heard. My sister—the cheerleader; the Bare Essentials salesgirl; the titian-haired goddess; the most popular girl at Adams Prep—was in love with some guy who didn't like her back.

No. No, that was just all wrong. That did not compute.

I sat there, trying to digest all this. It didn't make any sense. What kind of boy, asked out by the prettiest girl in school, said NO? She had said he was smart . . . well, how smart could he be if he turned down my sister? Unless he—

Suddenly, I gasped, as the full horror of what she was trying to tell me sank in.

"Lucy!" I cried. "Is it HAROLD? You like HAROLD MINSKY?"

Her only response to this was to weep harder.

And I knew. I knew it all.

167

"Oh, Lucy," I said, trying not to laugh. I knew I shouldn't have found the situation funny. I mean, after all, Lucy was genuinely upset. But my sister and Harold Minsky? "You know, Harold probably isn't all that used to girls asking him out. Maybe you, you know. Surprised him. And that's why he said he had other plans. I mean, maybe he just said the first thing he thought of."

This made her raise her head and blink at me tearfully.

"What do you mean, he isn't used to girls asking him out?" she wanted to know. "Harold's so smart. Girls must ask him out all the time."

Now it was REALLY hard not to laugh.

"Um, Luce," I said, not quite believing I was having to explain this to my older sister—the girl who had just informed me of an alternative use for the bathtub faucet, "not all girls are attracted to boys like Harold. I mean, a lot of girls like boys for their, um, bodies and person- alities, and not so much for their minds."

Lucy threw me an outraged look. "What are you talking about? Harold has a great body. Underneath those floppy shirts. I know, he spilled some of Theresa's paella on one and he had to take it off for her to put in the wash and I saw him in just his undershirt."

Whoa. Harold must have been working out or something in his basement, because if he had a good bod, it certainly wasn't from playing on any of Adams Prep's sports teams.

"It's just," she went on, "I mean, I watched *Hellboy*. I *told* him I watched *Hellboy*. And we had, you know, a nice conversation about how difficult it must be to defend others against the forces of darkness when you yourself are the prince of darkness. I would have thought, from that, that he would have realized—"

When her voice trailed off, I asked gently, "Realized what, Luce?"

"Well, that he shouldn't judge ME by the way *I* look," she said, her eyes very blue and indignant. "I mean, I can't help looking like *this* any more than Hellboy can help looking the way he does. I may look like a stuck-up popular girl, but I'm not. Why can't Harold see that? WHY? I mean, Liz saw past Hellboy's horns."

I had never heard Lucy speak so passionately about anything. Not even cheerleading. Not even Bonne Bell Lip Smackers. Not even Bare Essentials' new fall line of bikini briefs.

It didn't seem possible, but . . . she might

actually really be in love with Harold. I mean . . .
really in love with him.

I wondered if Harold has the slightest idea
of the feelings he's awakened in my sister's 34C
demi-cup underwire.

"Maybe," I said carefully, since a cheerleader—even an ex-cheerleader—in love is a
volatile thing, "you should give Harold the benefit of the doubt. I mean, maybe he *does* see the
real you, under your, um, horns, and just can't
believe someone as . . . horny as you would ever
like him back."

That didn't come out at all right, and Lucy's
wide-eyed glance told me I'd screwed it up, big
time.

So I said, "Look, maybe you should just ask
him out again for this coming weekend, and see
what he says."

"You think?" Lucy peered at me through
swollen—but still beautiful—eyes. "You think
he might just be . . . shy or something?"

"It's possible," I said. Although shy wasn't the
word for it. Oblivious, maybe. Or possibly afraid
Lucy had only asked him out as a joke. "You never
know."

"Because I was thinking it might be because . . .
because I'm so stupid."

"Lucy!" I looked down at her, my heart swelling with pity for her. Pity! For Lucy! The girl who had always gotten everything she ever wanted . . . until now, apparently.

Because the thing was . . . well, there's a really good chance she's right. About Harold not liking her because she isn't exactly class valedictorian. I mean, what do the two of them even have in common? Lucy is all about capped sleeves and Juicy Couture jeans. Harold's all about . . . well, megabytes.

"That can't be true," I said, even though, of course, a part of me thought there was a pretty good chance it could be. "I mean, you aren't, you know, *book* smart, like Harold. But you know a lot of stuff I bet he doesn't know. Like about . . . um—"

But the only thing I could think of that Lucy might know about that Harold wouldn't was, well, birth control.

"I memorized all those stupid vocabulary words he gave me," she said bitterly. "*Estuary* and *plinth*. Hoping it would make him realize, you know, that I'm really trying. I mean, I *want* to be smart like him. I *do*. Just like Hellboy wants to be good. But Harold barely even noticed. He was just like, *Good. Now memorize these other words.*"

"Oh, Luce," I said. "You know . . . you really should ask him out again. It may never have occurred to him that you like him . . . you know. The way you do. He may just think you like him as a friend." I hoped.

Lucy gazed unseeingly at my giant poster of Gwen in her wedding gown—taken from *Us Weekly* and blown up on the White House color copier—and sighed. "Well. All right. I guess I could ask him out again. God."

"God, what?"

"Well, I mean . . ." Lucy looked thoughtful. "Now I know how all those girls in school must feel."

"What girls?"

"The ones who ask guys out," she said. "And the guys always say no. I had no idea it felt like *this*."

"Rejection?" I tried not to look too amused. "Yeah. It can really suck."

"Tell me about it." She looked at the clock. "God. I have to do like ten more pages of vocab before I can even think about bed. Thanks for the pep talk, but I gotta motor."

I stopped her in the doorway, though. "Lucy?"

She paused and looked over her shoulder, her

face impossibly beautiful, in spite of the tears and the pieces of Manet's fur she hadn't picked off yet. "Yeah?"

"I'm glad you and Jack broke up," I said. "You deserve better. Even if he was, you know. Your first."

"My first," Lucy said. "But hopefully not my last."

"He won't be," I said. "And Lucy?"

"Mmm?" she said.

"You do realize," I added awkwardly, "that the same guy who played the Count of Monte Cristo played Jesus in that movie Mel Gibson directed."

It was finally Lucy's turn to look shocked. "He did not!"

"Um, yeah, he did. So, in a way, all those times in the bathtub, you've been——"

"DON'T SAY IT!" Lucy said. And then ran for her room.

I can't say I blamed her, either, really. For slamming the door so hard behind her, I mean.

Top ten things that suck about being the sister of the most popular girl in school:

10. When the phone rings, it is never, ever for you.

9. Ditto the doorbell.

8. The door to the refrigerator in the kitchen is completely covered in newspaper clippings featuring her. The only thing about you that's up there is a postcard from the dentist, reminding you about your six month's appointment.

7. She will never, ever be off the phone long enough for you to make a call.

6. Everyone expects *you* to want to be on the cheerleading squad, too, and then when you don't,

they act like there's something wrong with you.

5. She always gets to do everything first, whether it's go out with a boy, drive, see an NC-17 movie, spend Winter Break skiing in Aspen with a friend and her parents, you name it, Lucy's already gotten to do it, way before me, and probably better.

4. When people compare us to characters in John Hughes movies, Lucy always gets to be Molly Ringwald, and I always have to be Eric Stoltz. Who isn't even a girl.

3. There is nothing more demoralizing to a disestablishmentarian like myself than having to sit and listen to your sister's chipper voice reading off the morning announcements in homeroom during Spirit Week.

2. She gets elected Homecoming Queen. I get elected art room trash monitor.

And the number-one thing that sucks about being the sister of the most popular girl in school:

1. I can't even hate her. Because the truth is, she kind of rocks.

9

So I called him.

I don't know why, really. Well, okay, I guess I do know why.

And it wasn't because of Lucy's breaking up with Jack, and me realizing how great David is, in comparison with her loser ex. I mean, I've always known David is great.

And it wasn't because her impassioned speech about Hellboy made me more aware that the love David and I share—like the love Hellboy and Liz have for each other—is precious and a once-in-a-lifetime kind of thing. I already know all that.

No, the truth was, I took Lucy's advice. About the bathtub thing.

And it totally worked.

I mean, *way* worked.

And suddenly the whole idea of spending Thanksgiving weekend with David just started to seem a lot more, um . . . interesting.

Not that I was ready to say yes to it, or anything. His invitation, I mean. I was still totally freaked out by the whole thing. But I was definitely more . . . *interested* than before.

The only problem was that David, when I finally got through to him on his cell later that night, didn't seem quite as . . . *interested*.

Even when I explained to him that it wasn't him. It was me.

"Seriously," I said. "I want to . . . to . . ." I didn't know quite how to put what I wanted to do. *Have sex with you?* Or should I use his vernacular (SAT word meaning "characteristic language of a particular group or person") and say, *play Parcheesi with you?*

I found I couldn't bring myself to do either, though, and ended up settling for, ". . . spend Thanksgiving with you, David. Honest, I do. But think about what people would *say*. If they found out, I mean."

"Sam," David said, in a voice I might almost have described as long-suffering. Only what was *he* suffering about? Boys have it so totally easy. "I don't have the slightest idea what you're talking about."

Which was just so typically male of him.

"It's just that there's such a double standard if you're a girl," I explained. Or tried to explain. "Do you know what I'm saying?"

"Truthfully," David said, in the same non-interested voice he'd been using since he picked up the phone, "I haven't understood a single word you've said to me all week."

God. I had really hurt his feelings. I definitely had some apologizing to do.

"Seriously, David," I said, "it's just something I have to work through on my own. It doesn't have anything to do with you, really. It's like . . ." I tried to think how I could explain it to him in a way he could understand.

And suddenly, from out of nowhere, Deb Mullins popped into my head. Debra Mullins, in her tiny dance team miniskirt, and her big blue eyes, filled with hurt after another run-in with Kris Parks.

"It's like there's this girl at my school, and there's just a rumor she Did It—no one even knows for sure—and people call her all sorts of things to her face," I said. "It's horrible, I feel so bad for her."

"Um," David said. "Okay."

"I mean, what about at your school? The same sort of thing must go on."

"Uh," David said. "I don't know. I mean, I guess——"

"You *guess?*" My voice broke, I was so shocked.

"I don't know," David said. "I mean, I never noticed anything like that."

Oh my God. I couldn't believe it was so different at Horizon. But apparently, it was. Horizon must be like the Valhalla of private education, whereas Adams Prep is . . . well, hell.

"What about Right Way?" I demanded.

"Right Way? That dopey group your pal Kris Parks is in?"

"Yes," I said, not bothering to mention that Kris Parks is hardly my pal, since he already knew that. At least, he *should* know that by now, after the number of times I've complained about her to him. "Because it gets *out*, David." How could I make him understand? "No matter how discreet people are about it, eventually, it always gets out. And then they start in on you. Kris and the Right Wayers, I mean. Unless you're one of the elite——like Lucy. But I'm *not* one of the elite, David. Sure, I saved your dad and got on TV, and all, but I am hardly a member of the popular crowd. Or *any* crowd, for that matter. And I just know they'll be starting in on me next."

"Who will?" David asked.

Oh my God. I really did think my head was going to explode.

"RIGHT WAY," I said, through gritted teeth.

"But what do you care what these Right Way people say?" David wanted to know. "You don't even *like* them."

"Well," I said, "no. But——"

"Who are they to pass judgment on everyone else?" David wanted to know. "Are they the school's best and brightest?"

"Well," I said, "no, they aren't, necessarily. But——"

"I didn't think so," he went on. "Because if they were really all that smart, they'd know that abstinence programs, and all of that . . . study after study has shown they don't work."

I thought I hadn't heard him right. "Wait . . . what?"

"It doesn't work," David repeated. "Just Say No? Kids who went through Just Say No programs in school are just as likely to experiment with drugs and alcohol as kids who didn't, because those programs use hokey scare tactics no kid in his right mind is going to fall for. I mean, any moron knows you're not going to become a homeless crackhead from one puff of marijuana."

"Right," I said. Because, um, if that were true, all of the stars in Hollywood would be homeless crackheads. I've heard what goes down at those movie premieres.

"All those programs do is make people who go ahead and try whatever it is they're supposed to be saying no to—and believe me, more than half end up trying it—completely unequipped to deal with it," David said. "Like couples who've pledged not to have sex. All that happens is that they end up having sex anyway, only they don't use protection, because they don't have any on hand, because all they planned on was just saying no. See? It doesn't work."

I nearly dropped the phone. "Is that . . . is that really true?"

"What, you think the Centers for Disease Control made it up? Because they're the ones who did the study. So where those Right Wayers of yours get off, acting so high and mighty, I don't know."

"I don't know, either," I said, stunned by this piece of information.

"So . . ." David cleared his throat. "Are we okay now?"

"Totally," I said happily. Just wait until the next time Kris started in on Deb! I was definitely bringing up that CDC thing.

"And did you have a chance to ask your mom and dad about Thanksgiving yet?" David wanted to know.

Yes! And they said yes!

That's what I wanted to say. Well, what a part of me wanted to say.

But another part of me—a bigger part of me—was all, *NO! Okay? No, I haven't. This is a huge decision and even though I'm slowly coming around to it, I still need time. It's true I'm deeply in love with you, and I'm totally positive you're my one true love, but I'm only sixteen and I still have action figures on top of my dresser and I'm not totally sure I'm ready to put them away yet. . . .*

"Uh, no, I forgot," I said.

Hey, I kept my fingers crossed while I said it.

"Oh," David said, sounding only a little disappointed. Like, not as disappointed as I would have thought he'd be. "Okay. Well, let me know.

Because my mom wants to know how big a turkey she should order."

Whoa. Was that some kind of code for *I need to know how many condoms to purchase?* I thought about telling him he didn't need to worry about that part of it. But then my call waiting went off.

"That's my other line," I said, kind of startled because it was so late at night. I mean, the only other person who ever calls me on my cell is Catherine, and her parents make her go to bed at eleven on school nights.

"Okay," David said. "I'll see you tomorrow, anyway."

This kind of surprised me.

"Tomorrow?" Tomorrow was the Return to Family town meeting on MTV. "You're coming? With your dad?"

"Well, yeah," David said. "But we have life drawing before that. Remember?"

Terry! How could I have forgotten Naked Terry?

"Right," I said. "Yeah. Okay, see you then."

Then I switched over to the other line. "Hello?"

"Sam?" Dauntra shouted my name. From the background noise, it sounded like she was calling from a nightclub. Where a murder was being committed.

Which, knowing Dauntra, was not out of the realm of the possible.

"Dauntra?" I wasn't sure she could hear me. Where *was* she? Then I was hit by a horrible thought. "Oh my God, are you still in *jail*?"

"No," Dauntra said with a laugh. "I'm at a friend's house. Look, I just wanted to call and say thanks. For taking over my shift the other night. I totally owe you!"

"Oh," I said. "No problem. I hope you, um, didn't have too bad a time in jail."

"Are you kidding?" Dauntra said. "It was GREAT. I told 'em to keep my bunk warm for me since I expect I'll be back there real soon. But don't worry, I'll be out in time for my shift on Friday. Oh, right, you're going to your grandma's for Thanksgiving. Will you be back for your shift on Friday?"

"Uh," I said. "I'm not really sure. I might not be going. To my grandma's, I mean." I thought, once again, about asking Dauntra what she would do in my shoes . . . about going to Camp David, I mean.

But the thing was, I already had a pretty good

idea. What Dauntra would do, I mean.

Dauntra would Just Do It.

"I haven't really decided yet," was what I settled for saying.

"Well, it won't be the same without you," Dauntra said, just as someone in the background of wherever she was let out a shriek, and said, "Kevin! Don't!"

"Um," I said. "Is everything okay there?"

"Oh, sure," Dauntra said with a giggle. "Kevin just stepped on the pizza. Again."

I didn't even bother to ask what the pizza was doing on the floor. I sound like a big enough dork when I talk to Dauntra.

"So listen," Dauntra said. "I was thinking. We should do a die-in at work. To protest Stan searching our bags."

"Um," I said. "I don't know about that."

"Come on! It'll be fun."

"I'm not sure a die-in is the most effective way to get our point across," I said. I hated to be the one to burst her bubble, especially because in so many ways, I wanted to *be* her. I mean, Dauntra just didn't care what anybody said about her. I wished I could be like that. "The thing is, we might get. You know. Fired."

"God," she said. "You're probably right. Damn. Oh, well. I'll think of something."

"Okay," I said. "Well. See ya later."

"Yeah, see you tomorrow night," Dauntra said. And hung up, just as someone screamed, "Kev-IN!"

Which is kind of funny. I mean, that she said, *See you tomorrow night.* Because I'm not working tomorrow night. I have the town hall meeting on MTV.

Top ten reasons it rules to be a teen in the United States (as opposed to elsewhere):

10. It's unlikely you'll end up being one of the 250 million children worldwide between the ages of four and fourteen who work a full-time job (unless you have parents like mine. The only reason they're not making me work forty hours a week instead of six is because it's against the law. Thank God).

9. Three hundred thousand kids a year are forced to serve as soldiers in armed combat by their governments or rebel insurgents. With guns, and everything (although, seriously, what government would give my sister Lucy a gun? She'd probably use it as a hair straightening iron).

8. Corporal punishment was abolished here ages ago, but in many countries today, it is still considered perfectly acceptable for teachers to cane children for tardiness or giving a wrong answer (although this would so cut down on the level of goofing off at Adams Prep, we might actually learn something for a change).

7. One hundred thirty million children in developing countries are not in primary school. The vast majority of them are girls (and as much as I hate school, I do realize it's *necessary*. I mean, so you can, like, get a better job than one at Potomac Video. Because $6.75 an hour does NOT go that far).

6. In some parts of the Middle East and India, if you're a girl who gets caught flirting with some dude you met at the mall or whatever, your male relatives can murder you and pretty much get away with it, because of the perception that you've disgraced their family (which basically means Lucy? Yeah, she would never have lived long enough to flunk the SATs if she lived in Saudi Arabia or wherever).

5. Instances of girls as young as seven being forced to marry are common in sub-Saharan Africa, where 82 million girls will end up married before the age of eighteen, whether they like it or not—most of them not (in the United States, this only happens in Utah. And maybe parts of, like, the Appalachians).

4. Globally, an estimated 12 million children under the age of five die every year, mostly of easily preventable causes. About 160 million children are malnourished (and not because they're just eating Pop-Tarts all day like I would if I could get away with it).
   •

3. In Singapore, you have to get a special license to chew gum in public. If you don't have the license, and they catch you chewing gum, you can be publicly caned (although if people here in the United States had to get a license to chew gum, there would be a lot less cleaning up to do on the Metro).

2. In order to combat many of these rights abuses, the United Nations adopted the Convention on the Rights of the Child, a treaty that seeks to

address the particular human rights of children and to set minimum standards for the protection of their rights. There are only two countries standing in the way of the treaty being signed. One is Somalia.

The other is the United States.

Why? Because there's a clause in the treaty that suggests that girl victims of international war crimes be offered birth control counseling, and the religious right in the United States doesn't like that.

And the number-one reason it rules to be a teen in the United States:

1. Because this is still one of the few places on earth where you can mention how much something like the above sucks and not get thrown in jail for it.

Unless you're Dauntra, I mean, and you mention it by pretending to be dead in the middle of the street.

10

David got to the studio before I did. When I walked in, he was already straddling his drawing bench, arranging his pencils on the seat in front of him.

The minute I saw him, my heart did that flippy thing it does whenever David walks into the room. That thing Rebecca calls frisson. It got even worse when David looked up and saw me standing there, and our gazes met, and he smiled.

"Hey, Sharona," he said. "Long time no see."

And it was like there was this invisible bungee cord between us. Because I suddenly found myself being propelled toward him, until I was standing with my arms wrapped around his head, holding his face to my stomach, since I hadn't even given him time to stand up and hug me back properly.

"Well," David said in a strangled voice into the front of my shirt, "nice to see you too."

"Sorry," I said, letting go of his head—reluctantly—and lowering myself onto the bench beside his. "I just . . . I really missed you. I didn't realize how much until just now, when I saw you."

"Well, that's flattering," David said. "I guess." Then he leaned over and said, "I missed you, too," and kissed me.

For a long time.

So long that we didn't even notice the room was filling up with other people until Susan Boone herself cleared her throat, kind of noisily. Then we pulled guiltily apart, and saw that Terry was making himself comfortable, this time in more of a lounging pose, on the satin comforter Susan had laid across the raised platform.

Terry winked at me—I guess because of the intimate conversation he and I had had the last time I'd seen him—as Susan was fussing around with the comforter beneath him.

And I winked back, because, well, what else are you supposed to do when a naked guy winks at you?

Besides, it wasn't like I was freaked out anymore. About seeing a naked guy, I mean.

At least, I didn't think I was. I mean, I didn't feel freaked out.

But I guess I must have seemed freaked out, since about an hour and a half into our lesson, Susan Boone came over and asked me, quietly, if everything was all right.

I looked up at her, feeling kind of dazed, the way I always do when I'm concentrating on a drawing and someone interrupts me.

"Everything's fine," I said. "Why?"

Which was when it hit me. Oh my God! What if Susan wasn't talking about what had happened during our last lesson, with me freaking out over Terry and all? What if she was talking about something else—like how I was thinking about having sex with David? I mean, she's an artist and all, and way more perceptive than, say, my mom and dad, so she might actually have figured it out. Was that what she meant when she asked if everything was all right?

And if so, what was I going to say?

"Well, I'm just concerned," Susan said, looking at my drawing pad. "You seem to be concentrating so hard on getting the figure in, that you're completely neglecting everything else."

Blinking, I looked where she was pointing. I'd

rendered a highly realistic portrait, it was true, of Terry, in all his naked glory.

But it was also kind of true that he was just hanging there, basically in outer space.

"A drawing is like building a house, Sam. You can't start by hanging curtains. You have to build a foundation first."

Taking my pencil from me, Susan sketched in a background behind the figure I'd drawn.

"Then lay floors," she said, sketching the bench beneath Terry. Suddenly, he was no longer floating in space.

"You have to build your house from the ground up, starting with all of the boring bits . . . the plumbing and the wiring. Do you see what I'm getting at here? By going in and drawing all of this detail here"—she indicated the portrait of Terry—"you're decorating before you even have a house to stand in. You've got to stop concentrating so much on the *parts*," she added, "and instead, start seeing the image as a *whole*."

Susan, I realized, was right. I had been working so hard on getting Terry's face exactly right, I had neglected the other three quarters of the page. So now it was this huge piece of paper with a tiny head on it.

"I get it," I said. "Sorry. I guess I just got . . . you know, carried away."

Susan sighed. "I hope I didn't make a mistake," she said softly. "Letting you and David take this class, I mean. I thought you were ready."

I glanced at her kind of sharply.

"We *are* ready," I said hastily. "I mean, *I* am. And David is, too. We both are."

"I hope so," Susan said with a faintly worried air. She laid a hand on my shoulder as she straightened and then walked away. "I really do."

Not ready? Not ready for life drawing? As if! I worked furiously through the last fifteen minutes of class, anchoring Terry to a background, concentrating on showing the whole, and not the parts. I'd show Susan Boone who wasn't ready. See if I didn't!

But there wasn't enough time to really do what I'd wanted, and at the end, when it came time to critique everyone's drawings, Susan just shook her head at mine as it sat on the windowsill.

"You've rendered a highly realistic portrait of Terry," she said, in a kind but firm voice, "but he's still hanging in midair."

I had no idea what she was talking about.

195

What did she mean, I wasn't ready? Who even cared about the stupid background? Wasn't the subject of the drawing the most important thing?

Terry sure seemed to think so. He strolled over and was like, "Hey, are you gonna keep that?" and pointed at my drawing of him.

"Um," I said. I wasn't sure how to reply. The truth was, I had been about to wad the drawing up and throw it away. But I hesitated to admit it, because that would have been like saying I didn't think a portrait of Terry was worth framing and hanging over my fireplace—like he wasn't attractive enough, or something. And even though I thought he had a really weird job, I didn't want to insult him.

"Why?" I asked. Always a nice, safe answer for just about any occasion.

"'Cause if you don't want it, I'll take it," Terry said.

I was touched. More than touched. I was flattered. He liked my portrait of him! Despite the fact that it wasn't integrated into any sort of background.

"Oh, sure," I said, handing it over. "There you go."

"Cool," Terry said. Then, noticing that it

lacked the artist's signature, he went, "Could you sign it for me?"

"Of course," I said, and did so, then handed it back.

"Cool," Terry said, again, looking at my signature. "Now I have a drawing by the girl who saved the president."

I realized then that that's what he wanted— my autograph on a portrait of him, naked. Not that he'd especially liked my portrait.

But hey, I guess it was better than nothing.

"So," David said, coming up behind me at the slop sink, where I was washing charcoal off my hands. "You ready?"

I have to admit, I kind of jumped. Not because he'd snuck up on me, but because of the question.

"I still haven't had a chance to ask them," I blurted out, spinning around to face him. "I'm really sorry, David. Things have just been so crazy at home with Lucy and this tutoring thing—"

David looked down at me as if I had grown horns from my forehead, like Hellboy.

"I meant about the town hall meeting at your school," he said. "My dad said we're giving you a lift."

"Oh!" I laughed nervously. "That! Right! No, why should I be nervous?"

"No reason," David said, a twinkle in his mossy green eyes. "I mean, it's just MTV. Millions of people will be watching it. That's all."

The thing was, I'd had so much *else* to worry about, I hadn't really had time to think about it. What I was going to say at the town hall meeting, and all. I mean, I'd read the stuff the press secretary had given me, and even done a tiny bit of independent reading on my own, but . . .

The truth was, I was way more nervous about what I was going to do about the whole Camp David situation than I was about going on TV.

"Aw," I said. "It'll be fine. It always is."

Which is true. Going on TV with David's dad always had been fine, in the past. Not that we've done it that many times—I mean, it's not like we've ever paired up for *Crossfire*, or whatever. But I mean, like, at UN addresses, or the occasional fund-raiser that ended up being on C-Span.

And it had always worked out fine. I didn't see how tonight would be any different.

Until David and I pulled up to Adams Prep, and I saw the protesters.

That's when I knew the town hall meeting was going to be very, very different than talking to a bunch of rich oil tycoons in a hotel ballroom. Because rich oil tycoons don't generally have to be held back by dozens of police officers as they attempt to storm the car you and your boyfriend show up in.

Or wave big signs in your face that say KEEP YOUR NOSE OUT OF MY PANTYHOSE.

Or accuse you of betraying your generation when you try to get out of the car, shielded by Secret Service agents and police officers in riot gear.

Or try to hit you with an old turkey sandwich as you're rushing into your school, which, for the evening, has been turned into a battle zone—them versus you.

But since that's how it's always been at Adams Prep—them versus me—I wasn't all that fazed.

Except for the fact that I'm pretty sure that within that horde of screaming protesters I spotted a girl with Midnight Ebony and Pink Flamingo hair.

Top ten things that suck about going on television:

10. If you are a guest on a talk show or newscast, the person interviewing you will have cue cards or a TelePrompTer telling him or her what to say. You will not. You are just out there on your own. And if they ask you a question you don't know the answer to, too bad for you.

9. Seeing yourself on the monitor. Yes, that really is how big your head looks to everyone else.

8. The five minutes before you actually go live. You're sitting there, so nervous you want to puke, while everyone else runs around, having a good time. Because *they* aren't the ones going on TV. So what do *they* care?

7. The makeup and hair person. No matter what you say, he/she will come up with a look for you that in no way resembles how you actually look in real life, and that will cause your grandmother to call you afterward and ask if you meant to look like Paris Hilton.

6. The host and/or reporter will ignore you, except when the camera is on, and then he/she will try to make it look as if you are best friends. That is just the way it is. Move on.

5. No matter what you might have heard to the contrary, the food from Craft Services in the green room will mostly be composed of whatever you hate most . . . in my case, this always means tomatoes.

4. You will never get your own dressing room, but will instead have to share the ladies' room with two quilting bee finalists from Pennsylvania who will keep going on about how nervous they are until you want to scream.

3. Inevitably, someone at the studio will call his or her niece or nephew on his or her cell phone and make you say hello to him or her, because

you are the girl who saved the president, and the niece or nephew is a big fan of yours.

2. Then, when you get on the phone, the niece or nephew won't have the slightest idea who you are.

And the number-one worst thing about going on television:

1. Right after the camera turns off, and you remember everything that just came out of your mouth.

And you want to die.

11

"*I'm so* excited," Kris kept saying.

She didn't have to keep telling me. I could tell she was excited by the way she kept jumping up and down and squeezing my arm.

I guess I should have been excited, too. I mean, the president of the United States was going to be addressing the youth of America from my very own school.

But since I pretty much hate my school, it was hard to summon up any kind of enthusiasm over the fact that Adams Prep was about to get its fifteen minutes of fame . . . well, forty minutes, actually, if you factored in commercials.

Plus there was the small fact that outside the school were about a thousand people who really weren't all that jazzed about what we were going to say.

But Kris's conviction that her beloved alma mater was about to get its well-deserved due wasn't what had Kris so excited. And the protesters weren't even within her radar. No, she was practically delirious with joy over the fact that she was going to get to meet the president . . .

. . . not to mention Random Alvarez, the hottest VJ around.

"There he is," she kept saying, bouncing around beside me. "Look at him! He's so smart!"

Occasionally, she would say, "He's so hot." That was the only way I could tell who she was talking about. Smart meant the president. Hot meant Random Alvarez. Both men were in hair and makeup, getting ready for the show.

"It's too big," Random kept saying to the stylist who was trying to get him ready to go on. "It's sticking up too much!"

"That's how it's supposed to look," the stylist kept assuring him, as they both gazed at his reflection in a large hand mirror. "It's how all the kids are wearing it."

Random looked at me and went, "She's not."

The stylist glanced my way. I saw her jump as if a bee had stung her or something. Then she said, to Random, "Yeah, well, she's, um, doing her own thing."

Very nice! I mean, my hair doesn't look *that* bad.

Or does it?

The president certainly didn't seem too thrilled when he first noticed it. He took one look at my head, gave a kind of shudder, then went, in a sort of strangled voice, "Is that permanent?"

"Semi," I said.

"I see," he said. "And you're supposed to be . . ."

Do not ask if I'm supposed to be Ashlee Simpson, I whispered fiercely. Only I did it inside my head.

". . . punk?" the president finished.

"No," I said, surprised. I mean, how could he think I looked punk? I was wearing jeans, it's true. But also my form-fitting Nike shirt. Punk rockers don't wear Nike products. "I'm just supposed to be me."

"But—"

But David's dad evidently thought better of asking whatever it was he'd been about to ask, because he just looked heavenward, then turned back to the makeup artist who was blotting his nose. He didn't glance my way again.

Which just goes to show that you can't please all the people all the time.

Although you can please some of the people some of the time.

"I can't believe I get to meet you," the stylist I had been assigned was saying, as she tried to wipe the shine from my forehead. It is very hard to keep from sweating when you know you are about to go on TV. "You are, like, one of my idols. I loved the way you saved the president. That was so awesome!"

"Thanks," I said.

"It is such an honor to be able to work with you." The stylist's grin revealed perfectly straight teeth, the work of a really skilled orthodontist, or the product of pretty decent DNA . . . it was hard to tell which. "You are such a role model to girls everywhere. You know?"

"Gee," I said to her. "Thanks."

Some role model. I was seriously considering having sex with my boyfriend on a national holiday. Oh, and someone had just tried to hit me with a turkey sandwich.

"It's just too bad," the makeup lady said. I glanced at her sharply. Oh my God, had she read my mind? Did she *know*, somehow? About David and me? I'd heard about barbers who could read the minds of their clients just by touching their hair. . . .

"About this dye job, I mean," the makeup lady went on, fingering a loose curl of my hair. "You really should have let a professional handle it."

When she was done with me and my forehead shine, I went and sat in my assigned seat while everyone else ran around, going on about how nervous they were. Well, everyone else but Random Alvarez and the president.

"Oh, God," Kris said, coming up to me and squeezing my arm again. "Do you think he'd give me an autograph?"

"Which one?" I asked her.

"Either," she said. "Both. I don't care."

"The president will," I said, because I knew he would. "I don't know about Random. I never met him before."

"I'm going to go introduce myself," Kris said. "Before the show starts. Don't you think I should? I mean, I'm on the panel. It would only be polite to introduce myself. Don't you think? Just say hi, and welcome them to our school. It's the right thing to do. Isn't it?"

I shrugged. To tell you the truth, I didn't really care what Kris did. I had my own problems.

One was that I had seen my whole family sneaking into the gym a little while earlier, and seating themselves next to David and the first lady. My whole family—my parents AND Lucy and Rebecca. I'd hurried over to them and been all, "WHAT ARE YOU DOING HERE?" and my mom had looked at me like I was nuts.

"You didn't expect us to miss your little town meeting, did you?" she wanted to know.

"But you could have stayed home and watched it on TV," I pointed out. "I mean, it's *live*, so you wouldn't have missed out on anything."

"Sam," my mom said, sounding a little offended, "the president's speech is about how families need to spend more time together. Wouldn't it be just slightly hypocritical of us not to be here to support you?"

I hadn't thought of that. And I guess she was right.

But it was clear that, even though they were there, supporting me wasn't all that high on their agenda. My dad was on his cell phone—because somewhere in the world, a bank is always open—

and Rebecca was reading a book on chaos theory. My mom kept checking her PDA, and I saw Lucy craning her neck, looking around the crowd in the folding chairs for her friends.

But when her gaze skipped over Tiffany Shore and Amber Carson, I realized it wasn't her friends Lucy was looking for at all. It was Harold Minsky. Who wasn't there, probably because a town hall meeting from his school—even one over which the president of the United States was presiding—wasn't anywhere near as interesting as whatever was on the Sci-Fi Channel tonight.

But my family embarrassing me in front of everyone in my school—not to mention the nation—wasn't the only thing getting me down. The other thing I couldn't stop thinking about was . . .

Had that really been Dauntra out there? And if so . . . what did that even mean? I mean, does she hate me now, or something? Just because I'm supporting my boyfriend's father's initiative?

When I got back to my seat in front of the cameras—which hadn't been turned on yet—I saw that Kris had summoned up all her courage and gone over to introduce herself to the men of the hour——David's dad and Random Alvarez. She was pumping Random's hand as I watched, seemingly oblivious to the slightly annoyed look on his face. He was clearly still unhappy with his hair.

"Hey." David's voice tickled my ear. "Break an arm."

"Very funny," I said to him. He always tells me to break an arm when I'm about to go on TV, because breaking an arm was, basically, how we'd met——when I broke my arm saving his dad from being shot.

"Don't worry," David said, kissing me on top of the head. "You're going to be great. You always are."

"Thanks," I said, even though I didn't believe a word of it.

"And, hey," David said, still trying to cheer me up, "you get to meet Random Alvarez!"

"He's a total cheesehead," I said.

"Your friend Kris doesn't seem to think so," David pointed out. I looked in the direction he was nodding and saw Kris laughing at something Random had said (probably something like, "At least my hair looks better than that chick's, over there"). Kris put a hand out, resting it on

Random's chest, as if to say, "Stop! You're killing me with your wit!" But really, you knew she'd just wanted to touch his chest.

Random didn't look as if he minded too much, because a second later, he leaned down and whispered something in Kris's ear. She turned an interesting shade of pink, but nodded enthusiastically. Then Random slapped her on the butt.

Really.

I looked at David. "Ew," was all I could think of to say.

"What's up with Lucy?" David asked, nodding toward my sister, who was still looking for the love of her life in the many folding chairs along the darkened gym.

"She's looking for Harold," I said. I'd told David all about Lucy and her tutor in the car on the way over from the art studio. His response had been to nod sagely and say, "Oh, sure. She has a crush on him because he's the only guy in the world who's never paid the slightest bit of attention to her. You can see the allure."

I raised my eyebrows at this. "You *can*?"

"Well, if you're someone like Lucy, who's always gotten any guy she's ever wanted, having a guy *not* want you is a bit of a novelty. Of course she's going to fall for him."

I hadn't really thought about it that way. But it did make sense.

"It's a genius plan on the part of what's-his-name," David had remarked.

"Plan?" I'd scrunched up my face—but not in a repulsive, Brittany Murphy way, I hoped. "You think Harold PLANNED this?"

"Oh, sure," David said. "To get her to like him? Come on. It's brilliant. Pretend he doesn't care, drive her insane . . . he knows he'll have her eating out of his hand by the end of the week."

"Um," I said. "If you'd ever met Harold, you'd know . . . he's not that kind of guy."

David looked surprised. "Really?" Then he shook his head. "Poor Lucy."

Watching her now, as she tried to appear casual while she looked around for Harold, David said it again: "Poor Lucy."

You could say that again.

Now the director was calling, "Okay, people, we go live in ten. Places."

"Hey, listen," David leaned down to whisper in my ear. "I almost forgot. The weirdest thing just happened. My mom was talking to your mom just now, and she mentioned the whole Thanksgiving thing. My mom did. About you coming with us to Camp David."

Every drop of blood in my veins seemed to turn suddenly into ice.

"And your mom said it was fine," David went on. "I hope you don't mind. I mean, about my mom jumping the gun and asking before you had a chance to. But she really wanted to know. About the turkey, and all."

"And nine, eight, seven"—Random came and slid onto the stool beside me, with the president already perched on the one to his other side— "six, five, four—remember to look at each other, not into the camera—"

"Hope that's okay," David said, giving me a quick kiss on the cheek. Then he ran for his seat, just as the director yelled, "And we're on!"

And every camera in the room turned to focus on my horror-stricken, blood-drained face.

"Hey, this is Random Alvarez, and I'm here hosting MTV's latest town hall meeting," Random said, in a much deeper voice than he'd used before the cameras came on. He was also seemingly oblivious to the fact that half the student

213

population at Adams Prep, including Kris Parks, on a folding chair in front of us, was staring at him as if it were just the two of them standing in front of a minister in a Vegas chapel, about to be joined in wedded bliss.

"This is the show where you, the viewer, get a chance to hear about just some of the issues that are facing young voters in the upcoming election year. Tonight I'm proud to be joined by a man who needs no introduction, the president of the United States, who's here to talk about his new initiative, Return to Family. We're also joined by Samantha Madison, the young woman from John Adams Preparatory Academy— where we're privileged to be filming this show live right here in Washington, D.C."—screams from the students of Adams Prep, including Kris, who took that moment to shriek, *I love you, Random,* which the VJ ignored—"who risked her own life to save the president's, and was appointed teen ambassador to the United Nations for her efforts. Mr. President, Samantha . . . hello, and welcome."

"Hello, Random," the president said with a smile. "Thanks so much for having me here tonight. And may I just say, Random, that you are, like, totally my favorite VJ."

This got a nice laugh from the crowd. I saw the first lady, who was sitting beside my mother, turn to her and say something with a big smile on her face. My mom said something back, laughing.

I wondered how hard my mom would be laughing if she knew what I was *really* going to be doing at Camp David over Thanksgiving break.

"Thanks, Mr. President," Random said, in the same disturbingly deep voice. Also, I totally saw him scoping on Kris's underwear beneath her Talbot's kilt when she turned around in her folding chair to say something excitedly to the girl behind her.

"So, Mr. President," Random said, reading off the TelePrompTer just under the camera we all weren't supposed to look into. "Tell us a little about your Return to Family program, if you will."

"Certainly, Random," the president said. "You know, I feel strongly that with divorce rates as high as they are today, and the number of single parents on the rise, it's important we not forget that families are—and always have been—the backbone of America. If the family unit is weakened, then America is weakened. And I'm here before you tonight because I fear American families have been weakened . . . not just by the financial demands on them, but because of a basic failure to communicate. I understand the pressures on today's parents, who are working hard to provide their children with privileges they themselves may not have had growing up. But I also feel that parents need to make more quality time to spend with their children—not just cheering them on at soccer games, or helping them with their homework, but actual time, talking . . . opening the lines of communication between parents and children."

David's dad paused. He never has to read from notecards or the TelePrompTer. He always memorizes all of his speeches. It's something David can do, as well—speak in public completely extemporaneously (SAT word meaning "composed, performed, or uttered at the spur of the moment").

I, on the other hand, need notecards. I had mine, tucked in the pocket of my jeans. All I had to wait for was my cue, which Random was going to give me shortly. The president was going to go on about what parents could do to open the lines of communication between them and their children, and I was going to talk about what kids themselves could do.

Then, the day after tomorrow, I am going to go to Maryland and have sex with my boyfriend for the first time. Apparently.

"That's why I'm asking for a Return to Family," the president went on. "One night a month, where we all turn off the television, stay home from soccer practice, and just spend time with one another, talking. I know it doesn't sound like much . . . one night a month . . . can that really be enough to strengthen a family? Studies show that yes, it can. Children whose parents spend even as little as a few hours a month talking with them develop cognitive skills such as language and reading more quickly, test higher, and experience fewer instances of alcohol and drug abuse and premarital sex."

Wow. Maybe that was my problem. Maybe that's why I was going to be experiencing an instance of premarital sex. Because my mom and dad don't spend enough time with me.

Yeah. It's *their* fault.

"And you'll have the support of the American government behind you," David's dad was going on. "In an effort to help parents open the lines of communication with their teenaged children, I'm asking state legislators, as part of the Return to Family plan, to pass a bill that requires teens seeking prescription contraception at family planning clinics to have parental consent or to have clinics notify parents five business days in advance of providing such services to teens——"

There was a lot of applause when the president said this. Kris and her friends in the folding chairs in front of us actually cheered.

I didn't cheer.

I went, "Wait. What?"

But the microphone clipped to the collar of my shirt didn't pick it up.

Which was probably just as well. Because I couldn't have heard what I thought I'd just heard. No one else was reacting as if they'd heard anything unusual. I looked out and saw my dad getting up and moving out of the gym because he'd gotten another call on his cell phone. My mom was having a hard time clapping while also balancing her PDA. Rebecca was still reading her book on chaos theory. Lucy was putting on lip gloss.

Everyone else was clapping.

So it must be okay. I must have heard wrong.

So, wait. What was I worried about again? Oh, yeah. Sex. With my boyfriend. At Camp David. Day after tomorrow.

"I feel this is an important step," the president went on, after holding up both hands to still the flood of applause, "in opening the lines of communication between parents and teens. The United States currently leads the developed nations in teen birth and sexually transmitted disease rates. If parents were informed of their teenaged children's behaviors by the agencies that are currently allowed to keep this vital information from them—the clinics and even pharmacists that play a part in promoting teen sexual activity—they could effectively put a stop to it—"

More applause. *More applause.*

I couldn't believe it. I *hadn't* heard him wrong. What was happening? Why were people clapping? Didn't they understand what David's dad was *saying*?

And why had none of this stuff been in the literature the White House press secretary had given me? There'd been nothing there about requiring clinics and pharmacists to notify parents if teenagers came to them for birth control.

If there had, I'd have noticed. I mean, that kind of thing has *sort of* been on my mind lately.

The applause for the president's speech was thunderously loud. So loud that it was a few seconds before anyone heard me shouting, "Wait! Wait just a minute!"

Random, noticing that I'd jumped down from my stool, looked over at me and, not seeing from the TelePrompTer that it was my turn to speak yet, said, "Samantha? Did you, uh, have something you wanted to say?"

"Yeah, I have something I want to say." The notecards were still in my pocket. I wasn't pulling them out. I wasn't pulling them out because I'd forgotten all about them. I was too confused— and angry.

"What are you people clapping for?" I looked right at Kris Parks and her friends. "Don't you realize what he's saying? Don't you realize what's happening here?"

"Um, Samantha," the president, behind me, said, "I think if you'll let me finish, you'll find that what's happening here is that I am trying to strengthen the American family by giving parental control back to the people who know what's best for their children—"

220

"But that's . . . that's wrong!" I couldn't believe I was the only one in the room who seemed to think so. I looked down at Kris and the other kids from Adams Prep. "Don't you get it? Do you hear what he's saying? This Return to Family thing . . . it's all a crock! It's a trick! It's a . . . a . . ."

Suddenly, Dauntra popped into my head. Dauntra, who *couldn't* return to her family, because she'd been thrown out by them. Dauntra, who questioned authority—so much so, she was willing to get arrested for it.

"It's a conspiracy!" I shouted. "A conspiracy to take away your rights!"

"Now, Sam," the president said, in an easy voice, laughing a little, "let's not be dramatic—"

"How am I being dramatic?" I whirled on him to ask. "You're standing up there, telling the American public that you essentially want pharmacists and doctors to rat teens out if we come to them for help—"

"Samantha," the president said, looking a lot madder than I'd ever seen him, including the time I took the last chocolate-chocolate-chip cookie from a complimentary basket Capital Cookies had sent him. "That is an oversimplification of the

221

issue at hand. Americans have always valued the family above everything else. American families are this country's backbone, from the Pilgrims who came over on the *Mayflower* to the settlers who tamed the plains, to the immigrants who've made this nation the great melting pot that it is today. I, for one, will not stand here and allow the dissolution of the American family through the undermining of parental rights—"

"What about *my* rights?" I demanded. "What about the rights of the kids? We have rights, too, you know."

I looked back at the audience. It was hard to see their faces, with the bright lights from the show shining into my eyes. But I managed to find David.

And saw that he was smiling at me. Not like he was happy about what was going on, or anything. But like he understood that I was only doing what I had to do.

Because really, who else was there to do it?

And seeing that smile, I understood something else all of a sudden. Something that hadn't been at all clear to me until then.

"Don't you see?" I asked the audience—and the president, at the same time. "Don't you get it? The way to strengthen families isn't to undermine the rights of one member, while giving more rights to the other. It's not about the PARTS. It's about the WHOLE. It's got to be EQUAL. A family is like . . . it's like a house. There has to be a foundation first, before you can start decorating."

I wondered if Susan Boone was watching this. I sort of couldn't picture her watching MTV. But hey, you never knew. Maybe Susan *was* watching. If so, she'd know. She'd know that I finally got it. What she'd been talking about for the past two weeks, about how you couldn't neglect the whole for the sake of the parts. I got it now. I was ready for her life drawing class. I finally understood.

Too bad it was too late.

"Don't you guys get it?" I appealed to the other people my age in the audience. "The real reason the United States leads the developed nations in teen birth and STD rates isn't because clinics aren't notifying parents about their teenagers' behavior, but because here, all they teach us is Just Say No. Not, 'Here's what you do in case saying no doesn't work out for you.' Just . . . no. In countries where adults are *open*

223

with kids about sex and birth control, and teens are taught that there's nothing shameful or whatever about it, the rates of unwanted pregnancies and STDs are lowest—"

"I understand your concern, Samantha," the president cut me off, smiling a little tensely. "But I'm not talking about families such as those you and your fellow pupils here at this fine school belong to. I'm talking about families who haven't had the advantages yours has—"

I couldn't believe it. What was he *saying*? That families who lived in Cleveland Park were somehow immune from bad parenting and teenage sexual experimentation?

"—families who haven't taught their children the kind of morals your parents have instilled in you," the president went on. "You and all of your friends here at John Adams Preparatory Academy are great examples to this nation of the kind of children we should be striving to raise, children who have the moral character to stand up for what they believe in, to say no to drugs and sex—"

"So because I've said yes to sex," I declared hotly, "that makes me a bad example to this nation? Is that what you're saying?"

There was a beat as everyone—including me—realized what I'd just said.

As the knowledge that I had just announced to the entire country that I'd had sex with my boyfriend (even though I hadn't) washed over me, I couldn't help wishing that the gym floor beneath me would open up and swallow me whole.

Sadly for me, however, it didn't.

"Oh my God," I heard my mother's voice, breaking the sudden stillness that had fallen over the gym.

Then:

"Oh my God," I heard David's mother's voice say.

Then Random Alvarez seemed to come awake from the doze he'd sunk into while the president and I had been speaking, and said, into the camera, "And we'll be back, after these important messages!"

Top ten reasons the next time you're in a position to save the president's life, you might want to reconsider:

10. Everywhere you go afterward, you will be harassed by Johnson Family Vacationers.

9. You could get asked to go on *Oprah* and after saying no a million times, decide to do it to promote awareness of the issue of child slavery, which actually does exist, even in America, and then spend the whole time crying because Oprah asked about Mewsie, the kitten you had when you were ten who died of feline leukemia.

8. While working at your part-time job to make enough pocket money to support your lead

pencil habit, people returning copies of *Men in Black II* ask you if you know the real truth about Area 51, seeing as how you have an in at the White House, and all.

7. You will have to spend all of your free time in the White House press office, signing photographs of your own head for fans.

6. Don't even think about ever setting foot in a McDonald's again. You will be mobbed.

5. Everyone you know will ask you if you can get them the president's autograph.

4. You will find old past due notices from your local library that you thought you threw away for sale on eBay because everyone wants to own a piece of you.

3. You might fall in love with his son, and start dating him.

2. Which could make it extremely awkward when the president asks you to support his Return to Family program, and you find out that it violates

your personal right to privacy.

And the number-one reason you might want to reconsider saving the life of the president of the United States:

1. You might get mad at him and accidentally announce to the world on national television that you've had sex with his son. Even though you haven't.

Yet.

12

"*It's those* damned art lessons," the president said.

"It wasn't the art lessons, Dad," David said, sounding tired. I guess because he *was* tired. We'd been going back and forth about this for the past hour in our living room, ever since the president stomped out of the disastrous town hall meeting during the commercial break, causing MTV to have to put on a rerun of *Pimp My Ride*.

"All I know is my son wasn't interested in sex until he started drawing naked people," the president said.

"Dad," David said, "I've always been *interested* in sex. I'm a guy, all right? I'm just not actually *having* sex. Nor am I *planning* to do so in the near future."

Wow. I never knew David was such a good liar. Seriously.

"Then why," his father began, "did Sam say—"

"Wait a minute," my dad said. "Who's drawing naked people?"

"Sam is." My mom leaned forward to pour the first lady some more coffee. "Susan Boone asked her and David to take her adult life drawing class on Tuesday and Thursday nights."

My dad looked blank. "How's that supposed to have made them want to have sex?"

"We're not having sex," I said, for what had to have been the thirty thousandth time.

"Then why, in the name of God," the president said, "did you tell everyone in America that you've said yes to sex?"

"I don't know," I said. I had hunched myself up into the smallest ball imaginable on the sofa, hugging my legs to my chest, and resting my chin on my knees. "You were just making me so mad—"

"ME?" The president looked more annoyed than ever. "How do you think *I* feel? I'm standing there like an idiot going on about what a great example my son is, and it turns out the whole time he's been making me into the biggest hypocrite on the planet—"

"No, he hasn't," I said, feeling worse than ever. "Because we're not having——"

"Yeah, well, I don't exactly recall your asking me if I supported your whole reproductive health clinic parental consent bill, Dad," David said, at the same time. "In fact, I don't remember Sam seeing it anywhere in any of the Return to Family literature you gave her, either. Because if she had, I'm sure she'd have mentioned it to me."

"Parents should have the right to know what their children are doing behind their backs," the president declared.

"*Why?*" David wanted to know. "So they can act like you're acting now about it? What's the *point*, Dad? They're just going to freak, the way you are."

"If they find out BEFORE their child goes ahead and HAS sex," the president said, "they MIGHT be able to try to stop him, to open up the lines of communication so that they can keep that child from making the worst mistake of his or her life——"

"Let's not get too dramatic here, shall we?" My mom's tone was steady—the same one she uses in the courtroom. "Sam has apologized for what she did, and explained that she was speaking hyperbolically." (SAT word meaning "an exaggerated statement uttered in excitement.") "I think the real issue now is what we are going to do about it."

"I'll tell you what WE're going to do about it," the president said. "Boarding school."

David lifted his gaze to the ceiling with a bored expression. "Dad," he said.

"I'm serious," the president said. "I don't care if you only have a year of high school to go. I'm sending you to military school, and that's final."

I glanced, panic-stricken, at David.

But he looked calm . . . much calmer, as a matter of fact, than you would think, considering that he was about to be enrolled in some boot camp in the Ozarks.

"You're not sending me anywhere, Dad," David said. "Because I haven't DONE anything. Instead of jumping to conclusions like a reactionary, why don't you try to understand what Sam was saying during the town hall meeting . . . that there has to be a balance within families in order for them to work. Everyone is entitled to his or her rights, but only so long as they don't infringe on the rights of another. Just because

232

they aren't old enough to vote doesn't mean it's okay for you to strip teens of their rights."

David's dad glowered. "That is an oversimplification of—"

"Is it?" David asked. "You might want to keep in mind that in a few short years, those teens *will* be old enough to vote. And how kindly do you think they're going to feel toward the guy who made the law that rats them out to their mom and dad every time they want to buy a rubber?"

"Enough," my mother said emphatically, before the president, who looked madder than ever, could open his mouth. "We're not solving all of society's problems tonight." She sent the president her best courtroom look—the one her coworkers over at the EPA called *Death to the Industrialist.* "And no one is getting sent to boarding school. Let us, for the moment, be grateful that we have two smart, healthy children, who have always made the right decisions in the past. I, for one, intend to trust them to continue to make the right decisions in the future."

"But—" the president began.

But this time it was his wife who cut him off.

"I agree with Carol," the first lady said. "I

think we should just put this whole, unfortunate incident behind us, and try to look on the bright side."

"Which is?" the president wanted to know.

"Well." David's mom had to think a minute. Then she brightened. "At least our children aren't suffering from teen apathy, like so many of their peers. I mean, David and Sam really do seem to care about the issues."

The president didn't seem to think this was anything to be thankful for. He sank, with a gusty sigh, back down into his chair.

"This," he said, to no one in particular, "just hasn't been my day."

Suddenly—even though I was still really mad at him for trying to pull one over on me . . . because that's exactly what he'd tried to do, just as Dauntra had warned—I felt a little sorry for David's dad. I mean, after all, his program really *did* have some good points.

"Return to Family is a nice idea," I said, to make him feel a little better. "If it means, you know . . . this. Families talking stuff out. But if it means violating someone else's rights . . . well, how is that helping anybody?"

He gave me a very sour look. "I got the message, Sam," he said. "Loud and clear. I think all of America did."

Taking that as my cue that maybe David's dad had seen enough of me for one day, I crawled off the couch and slunk from the living room . . .

. . . and was relieved when David joined me in the silent kitchen, Lucy and Rebecca having long since been banished to their rooms . . . though I didn't doubt there'd been some surreptitious eavesdropping going on at the top of the stairs.

"You okay?" David asked, when we were alone together at last.

Instead of replying, I threw my arms around his neck and just stood there, my face buried against his chest, breathing in his Davidy scent and trying not to cry.

"There, there," David said, stroking my Midnight Ebony hair. "Everything'll be all right, Sharona."

"I'm sorry," I said, sniffling. "I don't know what came over me back there at the gym." I stood there with my eyes closed, enjoying the warmth I could feel through his sweater, wishing I never had to let go.

"Don't worry," he said. "You were just doing

what you always do . . . standing up for what you believe in."

It made me blink to hear him say that. Because it so isn't true. I *don't* stand up for what I believe in. Not with Kris at school. Not with Stan at work. And especially not with David. I mean, if I had, I wouldn't still be going to Camp David with him for Thanksgiving.

"Listen, David," I said, after taking a deep breath. "About Thanksgiving—"

"You're still coming, aren't you?"

Only it wasn't David who asked it. It was his mother, the first lady, who came into the kitchen at that very moment. David and I sprang apart.

What was I supposed to say? I mean, she looked really concerned. Like all she could think about was all that turkey that was going to go to waste if I didn't show up.

"Um, yes," I said. "Yes, of course I am."

"Good," the first lady said. "I'm so glad. Come on, David. It's time to go. Good night, Sam."

"Um," I said. "Good night, ma'am. And . . . I'm really sorry."

"It's not your fault," David's mother said with a sigh. "Tell Sam you'll pick her up Thursday morning, David."

David grinned at me. "I'll pick you up Thursday morning, Sam," he said and, after giving my hand a squeeze, dropped it, and followed his mother out into the foyer.

Thursday. Great.

"Well," my mother said, when we'd finally closed the front door behind our guests, "that was nice. Too bad they took their Secret Service agents with them. I could really use a bullet in the head right about now."

Even though I sort of felt the same way, I decided it was time to recite the speech I'd been mentally rehearsing since we'd all left the gym.

"Mom, Dad," I said, "I'd like to take this opportunity to thank you both for raising me in such a warm, supportive atmosphere, and for providing me with the kind of positive role models that a young girl such as myself really needs if she's going to make her way in this complex and ever-changing urban landscape—"

"Sam," my dad interrupted me, "I realize you were merely trying to make a point tonight. However, I think it's time we made some changes in this house. Some BIG ones. With that in mind, I would really like it if you would go to your room right now. And stay there," he added, sounding, for the first time in a long time, like he was actually doing some parenting.

"Um," I said. "Okay." And scurried up the stairs to my room. . . .

Where I found my sister Lucy waiting, her eyes wide.

"Oh my God," she cried, after making sure our parents had closed the door to their own room, and couldn't overhear us. "That was . . . that was . . . that was INSANE."

"Tell me about it," I said, feeling suddenly exhausted.

"I mean, I have never seen Mom and Dad so . . . so . . . so the way they were."

"Yeah," I said, staring up at my wedding photo of Gwen.

"So are you totally grounded?"

"No."

Lucy looked shocked. "Not at ALL?"

"No," I said. "But Dad said there were going to be some changes around here. Some BIG ones."

Lucy sank down onto my clothes hamper, clearly shaken to her core.

"Wow," she said. "You killed Carol and Richard."

"I don't think I killed them," I said. "I think

238

they just, like . . . trust me."

"I know," Lucy said, shaking her head. "That's the beauty of it. They have no idea what you've REALLY got planned. For the day after tomorrow."

I fully did not need the reminder. I clutched my stomach, suddenly convinced I was going to heave.

"Lucy," I said, "could we talk about this some other time? Because I think I need to be alone right now."

"I hear you," Lucy said, and rose to leave. "But I just want to say, for teenage girls everywhere, way . . . to . . . go."

Then she left, closing the door softly behind her.

And I looked up at Gwen, and burst into tears.

Top ten reasons I hate my school:

10. The people who go to it totally judge you by what you wear. If, for instance, you like to wear black, you are called a freak—to your face—by nearly everyone who passes you in the hallway.

9. If you happen to have dyed your hair black, you are not only called a freak, but a goth or punk freak as well. Some people also might ask you where you parked your broom, assuming you are a practitioner of Wicca, not, of course, realizing that Wicca is an ancient religion pre-dating Christianity that is based on the appreciation of nature and the celebration of life forces and has little if anything to do with brooms, which are only used as ceremonial tools in a few Wiccan rituals.

Not that I have ever studied Wicca. Much.

8. All anybody ever talks about is who won on *American Idol* or which school athletic team is going to which final. No one ever talks about art or ideas, just TV and sports. This seems exactly the opposite of what school is supposed to be about, which is opening the mind to new things and embracing knowledge (NOT of the latest Juicy Couture designs).

7. People totally litter. Like, they just throw their gum wrappers wherever. It's sick.

6. If, for instance, you happen to mention that you like a certain kind of music that *isn't* Limp Bizkit or Eminem, you are routinely shunned and called a ska-lovin' skank.

5. One word: P.E. Or is that two words? Well, whatever. It sucks. I hear in some school districts, they've started having cool things like self-defense classes and Outward Bound–type adventures in lieu of endless games of dodgeball.

I so wish I could go to a school like that.

4. Everyone thinks they have to know everyone else's business. Gossip is practically a *religion* at Adams Prep. All you ever hear in the hallways is, "And then she said . . . and then he said . . . and then she said. . . ." It's mind-boggling.

3. Even though everyone is so sanctimonious and holier than thou, it seems like the raunchier a reputation you have, the more popular you are. Like the football player who got drunk at that one party and Did It with a girl who turned out to be in Special Ed. He got voted Prom King that year. Yeah. Real nice role model.

2. The main hallways are filled with case after case of sports trophies, with only *one* case devoted to students who have won art awards, and that case is in the basement by the art room where no one goes but other people taking art.

And the number-one reason I hate my school:

1. My parents wouldn't let me stay home from it the day after I announced on MTV that I've said yes to sex.

13

Theresa had to drive us to school the next day, because there were so many reporters outside the house, my parents wouldn't let us take the bus.

Which was probably just as well, since, judging by the kinds of questions the reporters were shouting ("Sam! Were you and David ever intimate in the Lincoln Bedroom?"), the kids on the bus weren't exactly going to be super understanding of the situation, if you know what I mean.

Theresa, of course, was blaming herself.

"I should have known," she kept saying. "All those times he came over, and you told me you were studying. Studying. HA!"

"Theresa," I said. "David and I really *were* studying all those times he came over."

But it was like she wasn't even listening.

"What kind of example are you setting for your baby sister?" Theresa wanted to know. "What kind?"

"For God's sake," Rebecca said disgustedly. "I've got an IQ of one seventy. I know all about sex. Besides, it's not like I've never seen Showtime After Dark."

"Santa María!" Theresa said, to this.

"Whatever," Rebecca said. "It comes on right after *National Geographic Explorer*."

"I don't want to hear any more about it," Theresa said darkly, as we pulled up in front of the school and saw Kris Parks there, holding court by the Adams Prep Minutemen sign. "You girls meet me here when school is out. And no skipping class to have sex!"

"For God's sake, Theresa," I said. "I'm not a nympho."

"Just making sure," Theresa said. Then she drove away.

As long as it isn't raining, people usually hang around outside on the steps of Adams Prep before the first bell, talking about whatever was on TV the night before, or who's wearing what. Generally, if you aren't meeting someone on the steps leading to the school, you have to shove your way through the crowd to get up them.

Not today, though. Today, the crowd parted as if by magic to let Lucy and me through. As we trudged up them, clutching our books to our chests, conversations ceased, and voices fell silent, as everyone stared. . . .

Stared at the freak and her sister.

"This," I whispered to Lucy, as we made our way inside school, "totally sucks."

"What are you talking about?" she wanted to know. I saw her looking around the hall and knew she wasn't paying the slightest bit of attention to what was happening around us. She was just looking for Harold.

"*This*," I said. "Everybody thinks David and I Did It."

"Well," Lucy said, "aren't you going to anyway?"

"Not necessarily," I said, through gritted teeth.

Finally, Lucy glanced my way. "Really? I thought you'd decided to."

"*I* haven't decided anything," I said vehemently. "Everybody ELSE seems to have decided for me."

"Well," Lucy said, suddenly seeming to spy someone in the crowd she needed to speak to. "Good luck with that. See you."

Then she bolted . . . straight toward Harold, who was just coming out of the computer lab, his head buried in a copy of a book called *Algorithms for Automatic Dynamic Memory Management*.

The last book Lucy had left lying around in the bathroom had been called *She Went All the Way*. It was kind of hard to believe these two were a match made in heaven.

Sighing, I went to my locker and fumbled with the combo, aware of how all around me, the usual cacophony (SAT word meaning "a combination of discordant sounds") of the hallway had hushed as people dropped their voices to talk about me as they walked by. Eyes narrowed to heavily mascaraed slits as cliques of girls moved past me, and folders were raised over people's mouths as they whispered about me to one another. I could feel a million gazes boring into my back as I twisted the dial on my combination lock.

Why hadn't I faked sick today? How could I have forgotten that, fond as the American public might be of me on account of saving the president and dating his son, my fellow students at Adams

Prep have never liked me all that much. . . .

And now they have a brand-new reason to despise me.

And could I blame them? I mean, what had I done last night, really, except make their school look like a joke by announcing on TV that I'm no different than any of the public school kids they spend so much time looking down on?

God, it's no wonder none of them was speaking to me . . . that they were all whispering *about* me instead. . . .

"So. Were you ever going to tell me?"

I jumped, startled by the soft voice, and whipped my head around to find myself staring into the soft brown eyes of Catherine.

"Catherine," I said. "Oh my God. Hi."

"Well?" Catherine's eyebrows were raised. "WERE you?"

"Was I what?"

"Ever going to tell me," she said. "About you and David. YOU know."

I felt my cheeks heating up redder than ever.

"There's nothing to tell," I said. "Honest, Catherine. That whole thing last night—David and I have never—I mean, it was all a big misunderstanding."

Was it my imagination, or did Catherine's face fall a little?

"You didn't?" she said, sounding disappointed.

"No," I said. "I mean, well . . . not yet. I mean—" I broke off and stared at her. "Would you have *wanted* me to tell you? If we had, I mean?"

Catherine's eyes grew wide. "OF COURSE I would," she said. "Why WOULDN'T I?"

"Because," I said. "You know. On account of me having a boyfriend, and you—not having one anymore."

"I don't care about *that*," Catherine said, looking hurt. "You should know that. I mean, come *on*. Dish the dirt. Let me live vicariously!"

She was teasing me. I couldn't believe it. Catherine was *teasing* me.

I had never been so happy to be teased in my life.

"I wanted to tell you," I said. "I mean, that David and I were . . . you know. Talking about it. But I just felt like it might be . . . I don't know. Like I was bragging."

"BRAGGING?" Catherine grinned. "Are you kidding? You're like Amelia Earhart, Sam."

I stared at her. "I am?"

"Yeah. You're blazing a trail for nerdy girls everywhere. You have to tell us all about it. Otherwise, how else are we going to know what to do when it's our turn?" She snaked an arm through mine and said, "Now, start from the beginning. When did you first know he wanted to? How did he bring it up? Have you seen his you-know-what yet? And was it bigger than that Terry guy's?"

I laughed. And was surprised to hear myself doing so. I'd pretty much been convinced since last night that I'd never laugh again. Because who would be there to *make* me laugh, if no one was speaking to me?

I'd forgotten about my best friend, though . . . and in a way she, I knew, would never have forgotten about me.

"I'll tell you everything," I said, "at lunch. Not that there's a lot. To tell, I mean."

"Promise?"

"Promise," I said. And slammed my locker closed.

"So," Catherine said, as the first period bell rang. "See you at lunch."

"See you then," I said. Then added, to myself, *If I make it that long.*

249

Because I really wasn't sure I would. Make it until lunch, I mean. I am used to people poking fun at me on account of my clothes and hair. I mean, you don't go around dressed all in black in a sea of Izod and plaid without attracting comment, you know?

But this. This was different. People weren't calling me a freak or asking me what time the rave was. They were just . . . ignoring me. Really. Looking right past me, as if I weren't even there.

Only I knew they'd seen me, because the moment they thought I was out of earshot, I heard them whispering to their friends. Or, worse . . . laughing.

The teachers, at least, tried to make out like it was just another normal day at Adams Prep. They went on teaching as if completely unaware that the night before, one of their students had announced on television that she'd said yes to sex. In German, Frau Rider even called on me once . . . not that I'd raised my hand. Thankfully, I knew to say *"Ist geblieben"* to her *"Bleiben bliebt, und denn, Sam?"*

But still. It could have gotten ugly.

And then, at lunch, it did.

I was standing in the lunch line with Catherine,

pointedly ignoring all the people walking past us with a smirk—or, worse, a fit of the giggles—when Kris Parks and her gang showed up.

"Right Wayers," Catherine murmured, tugging on my sleeve. "Heading toward us. Four o'clock."

I felt my back stiffen. Kris wouldn't dare say anything to me. I mean, sure, girls like Debra, who are basically defenseless, she'll rip into without a second thought.

But someone like me? No way. She wouldn't dare.

She dared.

Oh, she dared, all right.

"Sssslut," Kris hissed as she and her fellow zealots passed by.

I had endured a lot already that day. The whispering. The snickers. The voices falling suddenly silent in the ladies' room the minute I walked in.

I had taken a lot. I had taken *more* than a lot.

But this?

This was just one thing too much.

I stepped out of the lunch line, and directly into Kris's path as she walked by.

"What did you just call me?" I asked her, my chin exactly level with hers.

There was no way Kris would ever say something like that, I knew, to my face. She was too big a coward. Not that I supposed she thought I'd hit her. I've never hit anyone in my life—well, except for Lucy, of course, when we were little. Oh, and that guy who'd been trying to shoot the president. But I hadn't hit him so much as jumped on him.

Still, Kris couldn't imagine I was going to hit her.

But she had to imagine I was going to do *something* to her.

If so, however, it apparently didn't bother her enough to keep her from folding her arms across her chest and, leaning on one hip, saying, "I called you a slut. Which is what you are."

Amazingly, loud as the Adams Prep cafeteria usually was, at that particular moment, you could have heard a pin drop. Just my luck that every single person in there chose that moment not to speak. Or rattle a fork. Or chew.

Or breathe.

That's because—as I should have realized—every single person in there had noticed Kris and her posse coming toward me. Every single

252

person in there knew there was about to be a smackdown. Every eye in the place was on me and Kris. Everyone in the vicinity had drawn in a breath when Kris called me a slut—"Oh, no, she di-n't!"—and was waiting for my answer.

Except that I had none. I really and truly had none. I had expected Kris to back down. I hadn't thought that, knowing she had such a large audience, she'd actually say it *again*.

I could feel heat rising up from my chest, along my neck, and into my cheeks, until I was sure that the blush suffusing (SAT word meaning "to fill or cover") my face was visible all along my scalp as well. Kris Parks had called me a slut. TWICE. TO MY FACE.

I had to say something. I couldn't just *stand* there in front of her. In front of *everyone*.

I was sucking in my breath to say something— I don't even know what—when Catherine, next to me, went, "For your information, Kris, it was all a misunderstanding. Sam has never—"

But even as the words were coming out of her mouth, I knew—I just knew—that the truth didn't matter. Whether I'd ever had sex or not was so not the point.

And it was time to let Kris know it.

So I went, completely interrupting Catherine, "What gives *you* the right to call people names, Kris?"

Which is possibly one of the lamer comebacks in history. But hey, it was all I had.

"I'll tell you what gives me the right," Kris said, making sure she was projecting (SAT word meaning "to throw or cast forward") her voice strongly enough so that the entire caf could hear her. "You went on national television and not only made a mockery of the president and the American family, but you also made a laughingstock of this school. This may come as a surprise to you, but there are people here who don't want to be associated with a school that allows people like you to attend it. How is it going to look now on our college applications when admissions officers see that we attended Adams Prep? What do you think they're going to associate our school with from now on? High academic achievement? Superior sports performance? No. They're going to see the name Adams Prep and go, 'Oh, that's the school that skank Sam Madison went to.' If you had any respect for us or this school, you would drop out now, and let the rest of us try to salvage what reputation we can for this place."

I stared at her, hoping she wouldn't notice the tears that filled my eyes. Which were, I told myself, tears of anger.

"Is that true?" I asked. Not Kris. But the rest of the cafeteria. I turned and looked out at all of the faces staring back at me. They all looked carefully blank.

Was this what the first lady had been talking about last night? Was this teen apathy at work?

"Is this really how you all feel?" I demanded of those blank faces. "That I've ruined the school's reputation? Or is that just how KRIS PARKS feels?" I whipped my head around to glare at Kris. "Because if you ask me, Adams Prep's reputation was never that great to begin with. Oh, sure, everyone *thinks* it's a great school. I mean, it's one of the best ranked schools in D.C., right? But that's the problem. Adams Prep ISN'T a great school. Maybe *academically* it is. But it's filled with people who mock you if you wear anything that isn't J. Crew or Abercrombie. People who don't hesitate to call you a slut to your face, whether you are one, or not."

I turned to face the rest of the cafeteria, my

voice having risen to an almost hysterical pitch. But I didn't care.

I just didn't care anymore.

"Is this *really* how you all feel?" I demanded. "That I should drop out? Do you really all agree with KRIS?"

For a second there was silence. No one moved. No one said anything.

No one except Kris, I mean. She tossed her head, and, looking out across the sea of faces, asked, "Well?"

Kris, you could tell, was enjoying herself. She's always liked being the center of attention, but she doesn't have the talent it takes to get roles in any of the school's plays or musicals. Calling someone a slut in front of the entire school is the only way she can think of to get the kind of attention she craves . . . well, that, and lording it over everyone on the student council.

When no one replied, Kris looked back at me and said, "Well, the masses have spoken. Or, NOT spoken, as the case may be. What are you doing, just standing there? Get out. *Sluts aren't wanted here.*"

"Then I guess *you*'d better find another school to go to, too, shouldn't you, Kris?"

That wasn't me. *I* wasn't the one who'd said that. I *wish* I was the one who'd said that.

But it was someone else. Someone who wasn't me or Catherine, who, by the way, was still standing there, open-mouthed, in the lunch line, her dark eyes as wide and horror-filled as my own.

No. The person who'd said that, about Kris finding another school to go to as well? That was none other than my sister Lucy, who'd scooted her chair back from the lunch table where she'd been sitting with her friends. Now she came sauntering toward Kris, a slight smile on her pretty face.

Though what Lucy could possibly have found to smile about, considering the situation, I couldn't imagine.

Neither, apparently, could Kris.

"I don't know what you're talking about, Lucy," Kris said to my sister in a voice that was considerably less snotty than the one she'd used when talking to me. Also, much higher-pitched. "This doesn't concern you, anyway. Everyone *likes* you, Lucy. This is about your sister."

"But that's just the problem, Kris," Lucy said. "Anything that concerns my sister IS about me."

As she said this, Lucy walked over to me and flung an arm around my neck. I suppose she meant the gesture to be chummy, but the truth is, she was actually strangling me a little, she was holding on so tight.

"And, by the way," Lucy added, "you're a liar, Kris."

Kris glanced over her shoulder at her gang, who all looked confusedly back at her as if to say, *We don't know what she's talking about, either.*

"Um," Kris said. "Excuse me, Lucy? I think we were all watching last night when your sister informed the entire world that she just said yes to sex."

"I didn't mean you were lying about *that*," Lucy said. "I mean wasn't that you I saw in the school parking lot last night in the back of Random Alvarez's limo?"

Kris stiffened as if Lucy had hit her.

And I guess, in a way, Lucy had.

"I . . ." Kris looked nervously back toward her gang. But they were blinking back at her, as if to say, *Wait . . . WHAT did she say? Now THIS is dishy.*

Kris turned quickly back to Lucy. "No. I mean, yes . . . I mean, I *was* in his limo. But we

258

weren't DOING anything. I mean, he just wanted to show me this demo he'd cut. He asked me to watch his demo——"

"And I guess," Lucy said, "you just said yes."

"Yes," Kris said. Then, she started shaking her head, realizing what she'd just said. "I mean, no. I mean——"

Suddenly, it was Kris who was blushing all the way to her hairline.

"That's not what I meant," Kris said, too fast. "It's not. It was perfectly innocent." She looked back at her fellow Right Wayers. "Random and I just talked. He really likes me. He's probably going to take me to the Video Music Awards . . . in New York City. . . ."

But no one believed her. You could tell no one believed her, not even her fellow Right Wayers. Because everyone had seen how she'd been flirting with him. Random, I mean.

"The thing is, Kris," Lucy said, still keeping her supposedly affectionate chokehold on me, "you have to be careful who you call a slut. Because the truth is, there are a lot more of us than there are of"—she looked pointedly at Kris's gang, and not at Kris—"you guys."

Kris stammered, "B-but . . . I didn't mean *you*,

Luce. I would never . . . I mean, no one would ever call YOU a slut."

"Let's get something straight, Kris," Lucy said. "If you're gonna call my sister a slut, then you'd better be prepared to call me one, too. Because if Sam's a slut, Kris? Then . . . so . . . am . . . I."

There was a collective intake of breath at this, as if everyone in the cafeteria suddenly gasped at the same time. My eyes, meanwhile, had filled with tears all over again. I couldn't believe it. Lucy was putting her reputation on the line for me. ME.

It was the nicest thing she'd ever done for me. It was the nicest thing *anyone* had ever done for me.

Until somewhere in the cafeteria, a chair was knocked over. Then a booming male voice called out, "So am I."

And, to my total astonishment, Harold Minsky strode up to us, his shoulders thrown back beneath his Hawaiian shirt.

Lucy's expression melted into one of utter devotion—tinged with astonishment—as she gazed up at her tutor, standing so tall and geeky beside her.

"If they're sluts," Harold said defiantly, pointing at Lucy and me, "then *I'm* a slut, too."

"Oh, *Harold*," Lucy said, in a voice I had never heard her use before—certainly never with Jack.

Harold's face was turning as red as the flowers on his shirt. But he didn't back down.

"Slut solidarity," he said with a nod to us.

Which was when Catherine suddenly stepped out of the lunch line, and, coming up behind Lucy, Harold, and me, went, *"ME, TOO,"* in the loudest voice I'd ever heard her use.

Oh my God! I craned my neck to try to see Catherine's face, but it was hard, considering Lucy's stranglehold on me. What was going on here?

"Cath," I whispered, "you aren't a slut. Stay out of this."

But Catherine just said, loudly enough for everyone in the cafeteria to hear, "If Sam and Lucy Madison are sluts, then so am I."

People buzzed at this. *Catherine*, a slut? Her parents didn't even allow her to wear *pants* to school.

Kris knew she was in trouble now. I could tell by the way her gaze was darting from us and back to all the people in the rest of the caf, who were still watching, as transfixed as if Simon Cowell and Paula Abdul were going at it right in front of them.

"Um," Kris said. "Listen. I——"

But her voice was drowned out as all over the cafeteria, chair legs scraped the floor. Suddenly, the students of John Adams Preparatory Academy were all standing up . . .

And declaring themselves sluts.

"I'm a slut, too," cried Mackenzie Craig, bespectacled president of the Chess Club . . . who had never even been out on a date.

"*I'm* a slut," shouted Tom Edelbaum, who'd played the lead in the Drama Club's version of *Godspell*.

"I'm the biggest slut of all," said Jeff Rothberg, Debra Mullins's boyfriend, his fists balled at his sides, as if he were willing to fight anybody who'd dare dispute his slutty status.

"*We're all sluts,*" the entire Adams Prep track team jumped up gleefully to announce.

Soon every single person in the cafeteria—with the exception of Kris and her fellow members of Right Way—was on his or her feet, declaring, "*I'm a slut!*"

It was a beautiful thing.

By the time Principal Jamieson got down there, we were all chanting it: *"I'm a slut. I'm a slut. I'm a slut. I'm a slut."*

It took the football coach to get everyone to quiet down. Principal Jamieson had to get him to blow on his athletic whistle—the one he'd taken the ball out of—long and hard, since no one had responded to the principal's shouted requests that we *Please settle down. Please, people, just settle down!*

No one could keep chanting through the piercing shriek of Coach Long's whistle, though. We had to clap our hands over our ears, it was so loud.

All too soon, slut solidarity was over.

"What," Principal Jamieson asked, when the chanting had stopped, and everyone had turned back to their food, almost as if nothing had happened, "is going on here?"

"She called my sister a slut," Lucy said, pointing at Kris.

"I . . . I didn't!" Kris's blue eyes were wide. "I mean, I did, but . . . I mean, she deserves it! After what she did last night—"

"She calls *me* a slut every chance she gets,"

Debra Mullins volunteered from the back of the room. "And *I* didn't do anything last night."

"Isn't it a violation of the John Adams Preparatory Academy's student conduct code to make pejorative remarks concerning someone's sexual orientation and/or alleged activities, Principal Jamieson?" Harold Minsky asked.

Principal Jamieson looked at Kris and her little group. "Indeed," he said sternly. "It is."

"Dr. Jamieson," Kris said faintly, "this was all just a big misunderstanding. I can explain——"

"I look forward to hearing your explanation," Principal Jamieson said. "In my office. Right now."

Looking chagrined (SAT word meaning "feeling uneasy or shamefaced"), Kris followed Principal Jamieson from the cafeteria.

I noticed that her little group of followers stayed behind, almost looking as if they were trying to appear not to know her.

So much for the part on Kris's college admissions apps about her leadership abilities.

Watching her leave, I felt like crying. Not because Kris Parks had been so mean to me, trying to humiliate me in front of the entire school—like I hadn't adequately proved I was capable of doing that all on my own, without anybody else's help.

No, I felt like crying because I realized how lucky I am. I mean, to have a sister like Lucy, and a friend like Catherine . . . not to mention so many people I hadn't even *known* were my friends, like Harold Minsky. I stood there beside them, my eyes filled with tears, going, "You guys. You guys, that was just so . . . so *sweet* of you. I mean, to say that you're sluts . . . just for me."

"Aw," Catherine said, patting my hand. "I'd call myself a slut for you any time, Sam. You know that."

Lucy and Harold weren't paying the slightest bit of attention to my heartfelt thank you, however. Instead, Lucy had taken Harold's arm, and was going, "Thanks for saying you were a slut for me, Harold."

Harold's face turned even *redder* than the flowers on his shirt as he replied, "Well, you know. I just can't stand idly by while a social injustice is being committed. I didn't know before that you . . . well, that you were such an insurgent." (SAT word meaning "rising in opposition to civil or political authority, or against an established government.") "I always thought you

265

were a bit of a . . . well, a follower. I guess I really underestimated you."

"Oh, I'm a TOTAL insurgent," Lucy said, giving his arm a squeeze. "I never get sick at the sight of blood."

Oh, well. Close enough, anyway.

"Listen, Harold," Lucy went on, "I know you couldn't make it last weekend, but do you want to go to the movies with me this weekend?"

"Lucy," Harold said, his voice sounding higher-pitched than usual—either because he was embarrassed, or because Lucy was kind of rubbing her boob against his arm . . . although I can't say for sure she was doing it on purpose. "I really don't think . . . I mean, I think we should try to keep our relationship on a, um, professional level."

Lucy dropped his arm as if it had suddenly caught on fire.

"Oh," she said, suddenly sounding as if *she* might start crying. "I see. Okay."

"It's just," Harold said, sounding uncomfortable, "you know. Your parents. They hired me to tutor you. I don't think it would be right, you know, for us to see each other socially."

Lucy appeared crushed. Until Harold added,

"At least, not until after you've retaken the test."

Lucy glanced up at him, looking as if she hardly dared to believe what she was hearing. "You mean . . . .you mean *after* I retake the SATs, you'll go out with me?"

"If you want," Harold said, in a tone which indicated that he couldn't imagine that, in a million years, she'd still want to. Go out with him, I mean.

Which just proved that Harold? He didn't know my sister Lucy all that well yet.

But I had a feeling, judging from the way Lucy's eyes were shining as she grabbed hold of his arm again, that he was going to get to know her *really* well.

"Harold," Lucy said, taking his arm again, "I can promise you two things."

Harold stared down at her, like a man in a dream. Then a grin broke out across the face that was as bright as sunrise over the Potomac (not that I've ever seen this, because who gets up that early?) and he said, "One: I'll always look this good."

Lucy grinned right back up at him. "Two: I'll never give up on you. Ever."

Wait a minute. That sounded kind of familiar. . . . *Hellboy*. They were quoting from *Hellboy*.

This, I could see, was a relationship that was going to last a long, long time.

"Well," Debra said, "that was cool. See you guys." Then she wandered over to where Jeff Rothberg was sitting, straddled him, and stuck her tongue in his mouth.

And I knew then that Adams Prep had gone back to normal.

Only this time, in a good way.

"Did you really see Kris Parks in Random Alvarez's limo?" I asked Lucy, after the bell rang, and we were making our way back to class. "Or were you just guessing about that?"

She was still sort of dazed with happiness over the whole Harold thing, so it was hard to get her to focus. But after I punched her in the arm a few times, she came to. "Ow. You didn't have to HIT me. Of course I really saw her in the limo. Do you think I would lie about something like that?"

"Actually," I said, "for me? Yeah. I think you would. Because Random's limo had tinted windows. There was no way you could have seen anyone sitting inside it."

"You know what, Sam," Lucy said, the tiniest of grins flickering across her lips, "you better duck into the girls' room and do something about your hair. It's totally pooching out in the back again, and it looks really stupid. See you after school."

And she disappeared down the hall, her pleated mini swaying as she walked.

And I realized I would probably never, ever know the real truth.

And I also realized that actually? It really didn't matter.

Top ten things you probably didn't know about Camp David:

10. Located 70 miles from the White House in the Catoctin Mountains of Maryland, Camp David was established in 1942 as a place for the president to relax and entertain away from the sweltering heat and humidity of Washington, D.C., in the summer.

9. Franklin Delano Roosevelt's name for the presidential retreat was Camp "Shangri-La" after the mountain kingdom in James Hilton's book *Lost Horizon.*

8. It was renamed Camp David in 1953 by President Eisenhower in honor of his grandson, David.

7. The camp is operated by navy personnel, and troops from the Marine Barracks in Washington, D.C., provide permanent security.

6. Guests at Camp David can enjoy a pool, putting green, driving range, tennis courts, horseback riding, and a gymnasium.

5. Camp David is made up of many different cabins situated around a main house. The cabins include: Dogwood, Maple, Holly, Birch, and Rosebud. The presidential cabin is called Aspen Lodge.

4. Camp David has been the site of many historic international meetings. It was there, during World War II, that President Franklin Roosevelt and British Prime Minister Winston Churchill planned the Allies' invasion of Europe.

3. Many historical events have occurred at the presidential retreat, including the planning of the Normandy invasion, the Eisenhower-Khrushchev meetings, discussions of the Bay of Pigs, Vietnam War strategy sessions, and many other events with foreign dignitaries and guests.

2. President Jimmy Carter chose the site for the meeting of Middle East leaders that led to the Camp David Accords between Israel and Egypt.

And the number-one fact you probably didn't know about Camp David:

1. It was about to become the place where I, Samantha Madison, would have sex for the very first time.

Maybe.

14

"*Would you* like more sweet potatoes, Sam?" the first lady asked me.

"Um, no, thank you," I said.

See, this is the problem with being a picky eater and going to someone else's house to eat. The fact is, there are very few foods I actually like. Thanksgiving is the worst. I mean, I hate practically every food the Pilgrims ever ate. I can't stand dressing. You don't even know what half the stuff in there really is, and the few things you *can* identify, such as raisins, are just gross.

I won't eat anything red except for ketchup and pizza sauce, so that automatically rules out anything else with tomatoes. It also rules out cranberries. And—UGH—beets.

Basically, all vegetables gross me out. So that means no peas or roasted carrots or string beans or—yuck—Brussels sprouts.

I'm not even a huge fan of turkey. I mean, I only like the dark meat. But everyone considers that part, like, the worst, so I only ever get offered pieces from the breast, which are white meat, which I can't stand, because even when it's cooked by a master chef from the White House, it's still sort of . . . gross.

In my family, it is understood that when it comes to Thanksgiving dinner, I'm totally cool with a peanut butter sandwich, which my grandmother always lovingly prepares with the crusts cut off.

Sure, my mom and dad used to complain because I wouldn't even *try* whatever they'd gone to so much trouble preparing.

But over the years, I've trained them to just leave me alone. I mean, it's not like I'm going to starve.

But this was my first Thanksgiving with David and his family. I hadn't really had a chance to train them yet.

So I just had to sit there and pretend to eat everything they put on my plate while actually just rearranging it in artful piles (I'd learned my lesson about trying to hide it in my napkin), while secretly intending to go back to my room and scarf down the plastic-wrapped peanut butter sandwich I had waiting for me in my overnight bag.

Right next to the spermicidal foam and condoms Lucy had given me.

Which I was trying not to think about.

David was clearly doing the same (trying not to think about sex), since one of the first things we'd done upon arriving at Camp David—after our ride to it on *Marine One*, the presidential helicopter—was break out the board games, on account of the bad weather (it was raining).

Not just raining, but *pouring* so hard that before David actually showed up to get me, I'd wondered if *Marine One* was even going to be able to take off.

Which hadn't been the only indication that Thanksgiving at Camp David wasn't exactly going to be a picnic. No, I'd also woken up with a big zit on my chin. From the stress. You couldn't really see it, but I could *feel* it. And it hurt.

I hadn't taken either of these—the rain or the zit—as fortuitous (SAT word meaning "good fortune or luck") signs. And it turned out I'd been right. At least, judging by how my day had gone so far.

I always thought—before I knew better—that our nation's leader lived in the lap of luxury. Like I figured the White House was this huge mansion, with animal-skin rugs everywhere.

And while the White House *is* pretty nice, it's *not* huge, and it's not as nice as, say, Jack Ryder's house in Chevy Chase. I guess it's nicer than the average American's house—you know, it has a pool, and a bowling alley, and all of that.

But the stuff in it that's the fanciest is, like, really old, and you aren't actually allowed to use it. Everything else is pretty much stuff you'd find in any house, like mine, or Catherine's. Just your average stuff.

And Camp David is even *more* plain. I mean, it's huge, for a house, don't get me wrong, with all these cottages spread out across all this land. And there's a swimming pool there, too, along with a gym.

But it's not *fancy*. I mean, the way you would think a world leader's country house would be.

I guess that's because our founding fathers were trying to move away from the idea of a ruling class. Also, the president doesn't actually make all that much money. At least, compared to my mom and dad.

Of course, David's family has money from the companies his dad ran before he became governor, and then president. But still.

Anyway, I'm just saying, Camp David is no castle. It's more like a . . . well, a *camp*.

Which makes it kind of a weird place for someone to lose her virginity.

Or *not* lose it, as the case may be. Because I had given it a lot of thought over the past twenty-four hours, and the truth was, I wasn't.

Ready, I mean.

Yes, I know I'd been practicing. A lot. A *lot*.

And, yes, I *know* I had said I was on national (okay, cable) television. I know everyone in the entire country—including my own grandma, no doubt—thinks I'm sexually active.

And I know the worst had already happened—being publicly accused of being a slut by Kris Parks—and I'd already weathered that just fine.

But just because everyone thinks I've already Done It isn't a good enough reason to Do It. I mean, it's still this incredibly huge step. With sex comes great responsibility. An end of innocence.

Not to mention possible STDs and unwanted pregnancy. Who needs the aggravation?

Especially when, let's face it, high school is aggravation enough as it is.

So, I had made my decision.

Now I just had to break the news to David.

Which might have been another reason I had so much trouble actually getting anything down at dinner. I mean, David had to think he was Getting Some tonight. He *had* to. I'd seen the twinkle in his eye when he'd broken out the Parcheesi board (Yes! An actual Parcheesi board!) earlier that afternoon. He'd all but winked at me over the dice cup.

I was going to be crushing all of his adolescent dreams. He was going to hate me.

No wonder I couldn't eat.

I was really relieved when the first lady excused David and me, and we went into the living room to watch the new Adam Sandler (yes, the president *does* get first-run movies before they ever go on sale for anyone else). That took my mind off what I knew was going to happen after everyone else went to bed. Sort of. Up until the moment the movie ended, and next thing I knew, David was walking me to the door of my bedroom——which was in the main part of the house, not one of the cottages——and saying, "Good night, Sam." In this kind of voice. This kind of "this is for my parents' benefit" voice.

Because he knew neither of us would *really* be going to sleep.

Anytime soon.

Or so he thought.

I felt totally panicky as I closed the door to my room behind me. My room was a pretty good example of how *not* fancy the presidential retreat is. It was just this ordinary room, white with wood paneling and a navy blue bedspread over a queen-sized bed. There were bookshelves on the wall filled with books about——I am not kidding you——birds and bird-watching. It had its own bathroom and a view of the lake. But really, that was about all it had going for it.

But this room, apparently, was the place where David thought we were going to Do It. After everyone else had gone to sleep, and David came back.

Which might explain why suddenly I felt so . . .

Nauseous.

And it wasn't just all the marshmallow from

the top of the sweet potatoes, either.

The peanut butter sandwich helped a little.

But after I'd eaten it, I didn't know what to do. I mean, I couldn't start getting ready for bed, or anything, because who knew what the sight of me in my pajamas might do to David? Inflame his senses, or whatever, and make it even harder on him when I said no. Not that my pajamas were very sexy, or anything, being flannel, with pictures of suitcases on them, under the words *Bon Voyage* written all over (my grandma had gotten them for me for my birthday last year, for when I traveled as teen ambassador to the UN).

No, it was much better to remain fully clothed. So I did. I sat down on the edge of my bed and waited. It wouldn't be long now. David would be showing up any second. As soon as he was sure his parents were safely asleep. It was past midnight, so he had to be coming soon. Presidents get up way early, so surely his mom and dad had already hit the hay. He would be coming any minute.

Any minute now.

And I was ready for him. I had my speech all planned out. "David," I would say, gazing tenderly into his eyes, "you know I love you. And I know I said on national (cable) television the other night that I was ready to say yes to sex. But the fact is, I'm not. I know you love me enough to understand, and that you'll wait for me. Because that's what real love is . . . being willing to wait."

Actually I got that last part from this pin the Right Wayers had been giving out at lunch a couple of weeks ago. It was a pin in the shape of a heart that said *Love Means . . . Willing to Wait*. At the time, I had made gagging noises for Catherine's benefit when I'd read it.

But now it was sort of starting to make sense.

I wished I hadn't taken that pin and stabbed it through the chest of the *Nightmare Before Christmas* Sally action figure at work. I could have used it now. I could give it to David, as a symbol of my commitment to have sex with him some-day. Some day *other* than today.

I could totally picture myself giving it to him, and maybe saying something really memorable and touching. Maybe something like, "'Hey, you on the other side. Let her go. 'Cause for her, I'll cross over, and when that happens, you'll be sorry.'"

It really seemed to me like a situation that was

crying out for a quote from *Hellboy*.

Anyway, I was ready. I had brushed my teeth—just so my breath wouldn't offend as I gently let him down—and examined my zit. No improvement. The good news, though, was that you still couldn't see it, even without makeup. I could just *feel* it, all sore and angry at me. I don't actually wear that much makeup, just mascara and cover-up mostly, and a little lip gloss. Still, I figured I should keep it on for the Big Gentle Let Down, so at least my eyelashes would be the same color as my hair. It just seemed like, you know, I should try to look my best for The Big Sex Talk, even though David has seen me looking *far* from my best more times than I can count.

Yep. I was ready. Ready and waiting. Just one thing was missing.

David.

Speaking of which . . . where *was* he? It had been nearly an hour since we'd all gone off to bed. It was almost twelve thirty now.

Suddenly, I started feeling nauseous in a different way. Had David changed his mind? Had I done something to make him not want to have sex with me? Was it my zit? Had he noticed it?

But it seemed highly unlikely a guy would

change his mind about having sex with his girl-friend over a zit.

But wait a minute. I didn't even *want* to have sex with him. So what did I care?

Was it something else, then? Was it what had happened on MTV? Oh my God, had my announcing I'd said Yes to Sex on national (cable) television killed the spontaneity or something? They are always going on about how sex should be spontaneous in *Cosmo.* Had I somehow ruined that?

Well, what if I had? Good. I don't want to Do It, anyway.

But this didn't seem very likely, either. Sex isn't the same kind of big deal to boys that it is to girls. Or at least it doesn't seem that way. Oh, sure, boys all *want* to have sex. But they don't *obsess* over it the way we do. They just *do* it.

At least, that's how it seems in movies, like *American Pie.*

So where *was* he? This waiting around was *killing* me. I just wanted to tell him I wasn't going to Do It and get it over with already.

I waited for five more minutes. Still no David.

What if something had happened to him? What if he'd tripped in the shower and hit his head and was lying there unconscious with his mouth open, his lungs filling up with water even as I was sitting here?

Worse, what if David had simply changed his mind?

HOW COULD HE CHANGE HIS MIND AFTER I'D BEEN DOING ALL THAT PRACTICING?

Before I even knew what I was doing, I was on my feet and storming for the door. How dare he? How DARE he change his mind after putting me through what he'd put me through all week? HE wasn't going to be the one to decide we weren't having sex after all. *I* was the one who was going to decide that. I had already decided that, long before he had.

I charged down the dark, empty hallway, thinking of all the things I was going to say to him—or not say to him. He certainly wasn't getting any *Hellboy* quotes out of me now. No way. He'd had his opportunity for *Hellboy* quotes and completely wasted it. No more *Love Means . . . Willing to Wait* for him. He was going to get *Bon Voyage*. That was what he was going to get.

When I got to David's room, I could see light shining out from the crack under his door. So he was still up. He was still up! He just hadn't bothered to move his lazy butt on down the hall to let me know we weren't having sex after all. Yeah, thanks! Thanks for letting me know! Who knows how long I would have stayed up, waiting to say no to sex, before I realized he wasn't even coming?

Which was why I threw open his door without even knocking, and stood there, glaring at him, my chest heaving. But not in a romance novel kind of a way. More in an I'm Going to Kill You kind of way.

David looked up from the book he was reading in bed.

A book on architecture.

While I, his girlfriend, had been sitting for what seemed like hours, waiting for him to come deflower me already.

David seemed more than a little surprised to see me. You know, considering.

"Sam," he said, closing the book—but leaving, I couldn't help noticing, his finger inside it, to hold his place, "is everything all right? You're not sick or something, are you?"

Seriously. I almost lost it, then and there.

"Sick?" I echoed. "SICK? Yes, I'm sick. Sick of WAITING for you."

This made him take his finger out from the book and actually set it aside. He looked concerned.

He also, I couldn't help noticing, looked totally hot. Mostly because he didn't happen to be wearing a shirt. But also because, let's face it: David always looks hot.

"Waiting for me?" David, looking genuinely perplexed, wanted to know. "Waiting for me for what?"

I couldn't believe it. I COULDN'T BELIEVE HE WAS ASKING ME THIS. Hot or not, what kind of question was this?

"TO HAVE SEX," I almost yelled.

Only I didn't want to wake his parents up. Let alone the Secret Service.

So I whispered it.

Loudly.

But even though I whispered it, instead of shouting it, David still looked totally shocked. His face, in the warm light from the reading lamp beside his bed, started to turn as red as my hair used to be.

"Sex?" he echoed hoarsely.

"You know what I'm talking about," I said. I couldn't believe this. What was *wrong* with him?

"You're the one who brought it up."

"*I did?*" His voice kind of broke on the word *did*. "When?"

"Outside my house," I said impatiently. What was wrong with him?

Maybe he really had slipped and hit his head in the shower. "Remember? You invited me to Camp David to play Parcheesi."

"Yeah," David said, now looking blank. But also still hot. "Which we did already."

Which we did already. Oh my God. I couldn't believe he'd said that.

Also, that he'd still looked so hot saying it.

"But I didn't mean . . ." David stammered. "I mean, when I said Parcheesi, I meant—"

Something cold gripped my heart. Seriously. It was like someone had dumped a whole glass of ice water over my head, and a bunch of cubes had slid down my shirt.

Because it was obvious by the expression on David's face—not to mention, the way he was acting—that when he'd said Parcheesi, he'd really meant . . . Parcheesi.

"But," I said, in a small voice, "you . . . you said you thought we were ready."

"Ready to spend the weekend together with

287

my parents," David said, his own voice uncharacteristically squeaky. "That's all I meant by ready." Then, his eyes widening, he went, "Is THAT what you were talking about the other night? When you said you've said yes to sex?"

"Well, yeah," I said. "What did you *think* I meant?"

David kind of shrugged. "I just thought you were trying to make a point to my dad. That's all. I didn't know you were REALLY . . . you know. Saying yes to sex."

Especially since he hadn't even asked me.

"Oh," I said.

And wanted to die.

Because it had all been for nothing. All of it, the worrying, the long talks with Lucy, the Just Say Yes to Sex thing, slut solidarity—all of it, for nothing.

Because David had never meant for us to have sex this weekend. *I* was the one who'd jumped to the conclusion that Parcheesi meant sex. *I* was the one who'd assumed when David had said he thought we were ready, he'd meant he thought we were ready for sex. *I* was the one who'd said yes to sex, when it turned out no one had even *asked* me.

It had all been me. I had brought all that worry and angst upon myself.

For nothing.

God. How totally embarrassing.

"Um," I said. Now *I* was the one turning red. I mean, what could he be thinking about me? Here I'd come, barging into his room, demanding to know why we weren't having sex already. He must think I'm a total raving lunatic. "Yeah. Listen. Um. I'll just, um, be going."

Except with each step back toward the door, I couldn't help noticing stuff. Like how good David looked in the glow of the lamplight.

And how green his eyes were, the exact color of the lawn at the Kentucky Derby.

And how he still looked so confused, in an adorable, geeky-boy kind of way, with his hair kind of sticking up in back, where it had gotten mushed against the headboard as he was reading.

And how wide and comfy-looking his chest was, and how good it would feel to rest my head there, and listen to his heartbeat. . . .

And suddenly, I heard myself say, "Um, could you just wait here a second?"

Like he was going somewhere.

Then I turned around and ran as fast as I

could back to my room.

When I came back, I was even *more* out of breath.

I was also holding a brown paper bag.

David glanced at it, then up at me.

"Sam," he said, in a suspicious—but not necessarily displeased—voice. "What's in the bag?"

So I showed him.

15

When I let myself into the house the next day, I was shocked to see my father sitting in the living room, listening to Rebecca play "New York, New York" on her clarinet.

"What are *you* doing here?" I blurted out, as Manet, who'd run to the door at the sound of my key in the lock, jumped all over me.

Rebecca lowered her instrument and said, "Excuse me. I'm still *playing*."

"Oh," I said, taken aback. "Sorry."

My dad, who wasn't reading the paper, talking on the phone, or doing anything, actually, except apparently listening to his youngest daughter's performance, smiled at me a little painfully as I stood there waiting for the song to end. When it did, he clapped, almost as if he'd really enjoyed it.

"That was great," he said enthusiastically.

"Thank you." Rebecca primly turned a page of the book sitting on her music stand. "And now, continuing my tribute to the nation's greatest cities, I will play the song 'Gary, Indiana' from *The Music Man*."

"Uh, could you wait until I've gotten a refill?" my dad asked, holding up his empty coffee mug. Then he hurried out into the kitchen.

I looked at Rebecca.

"What," I asked her, "is going on here?"

"Those Big Changes Dad was talking about the night you said yes to sex on TV," she said with a shrug. "They've decided to spend more time with us. So I'm going to play him every single song in my repertoire, to see how long until he cracks. He's held up surprisingly well, so far. I give him two more songs."

Stunned, I carried my overnight bag into the kitchen, lured there by the smell of something baking. I was shocked to see my mom, and not Theresa, bent over the open oven door, going, "Do these look done to you, honey?" to my dad, who was refilling his coffee mug.

She was baking chocolate chip cookies. My *mother*, the meanest environmental lawyer in

292

town, was baking chocolate chip cookies. Her PDA was nowhere in sight.

My overnight bag fell from my hands and landed with a thump on the floor.

My mom looked over her shoulder at me and smiled.

"Oh, Sam," she said. "What are you doing home? I thought you were gone for the weekend."

"We had to come back early," I said. "David's dad wanted to get together with his advisors to revise some things on his Return to Family initiative before unveiling it to Congress on Monday. What are you *doing*?"

"Baking cookies, honey," she said, and pulled the tray from the oven, then closed the door. "Watch out, they're hot!" This she said to my dad as he tried to reach for one.

"Why aren't you guys still at Grandma's?" I asked.

"That woman is dead to me," my dad said, taking a cookie anyway, and burning his fingers.

"Richard," my mother said, narrowing her eyes at him. To me, she said, "Your father and his mother had a little disagreement, so we came home early."

"Little?" my dad said, after gulping some coffee to wash down the hot cookie he'd stuffed in his mouth, to keep it from burning his fingers, and burning his tongue instead. "There was nothing little about it."

"Richard," Mom said. "Richard, I told you, those cookies are *hot*."

My dad took two more anyway, holding them on a paper towel. "See ya," he said, heading back toward the living room, Manet following eagerly behind him, in hopes of scoring some dropped cookie. "'Gary, Indiana' awaits."

"Okay, seriously." I stared at my mom. "What is going on here? I leave for one night, and you guys suddenly turn into the Cleavers? Where's Theresa?"

"I gave her the weekend off," my mom said, attempting to scrape the cookies she'd just baked off the metal tray they were sitting on. Unfortunately, they weren't coming off all that easily. "It's important for her to spend time with her own family, you know. Just like it's important for all of us to spend time together, too. Your father and I discussed it, and we agree with the president. Not with *everything* he said, of course." She worked at scraping up a particularly recalcitrant (SAT word meaning "stubborn or rebellious") cookie.

"But it's time we started spending more time with you girls," she went on. "Your father thinks maybe Lucy would study more if we kept an eye on her. And you know what Rebecca's teachers say about her need for more socialization. That's why both your father and I will be cutting back our hours at the office. True, it will mean less money coming in. That's what your father's fight with his mother was about." My mom grimaced. "But then, I was never that enthusiastic about going to Aruba for Christmas with her anyway."

I just stared at her, barely able to register what I'd just heard. Mom and Dad were going to be spending more time with us?

Was this a good thing? Or a bad thing? Or a *very* bad thing?

"What about me?" I croaked.

"What about you, honey?" my mom asked.

"Well, I mean . . . is this about my detention last week? Or what I said on TV?"

"Oh, honey." My mom smiled at me. "You know we don't worry all that much about you, Sam. You've always had such a good head on your shoulders." Then she added briskly, "But I do imagine if I'm home more, I might at least be able to keep you from doing anything else to your poor hair."

She smiled to show she was joking . . . only I could tell she wasn't *really*.

"Huh," I said. "Great."

Like someone in a daze, I headed up the stairs to my room. My dad had promised there'd be some BIG changes around our house.

I just never imagined they'd be *this* big.

I was in so much shock, I didn't even hear Lucy when she called to me from her room as I passed by her open door. It was only the second time she screeched, "SAM!" that I realized she was talking to me, and poked my head into her room to see what she wanted.

"You're back early!" Lucy cried, from where she was perched under the big canopy over her bed, perusing the latest *Vogue*, or whatever.

"So are you," I said. "Did Dad and Grandma really get into it?"

"Totally," Lucy said. "Well, you know how they are. They'll be speaking again by Monday. At least, I hope so, because I was totally getting a new bikini for Aruba. So . . . how did it go?"

"Fine," I said, conscious of the fact that Lucy

has the long-term memory of a cat, and that it was unlikely she'd remember our conversation from the week before, or even that she'd ever bought me birth control.

But I guess our conversation had been more important to her than I'd thought—either that, or Harold's tutoring had improved her memory—because she went, "Come in, come in and tell me all about, you know. *It*," in a conspiratorial voice.

I slipped inside her room and closed the door so no one downstairs could overhear our conversation—not that that was very likely anyway, considering the volume at which Rebecca was playing her clarinet.

"So," Lucy said, patting the empty spot beside her on the mattress. "What happened? With David, I mean? Did you two, you know, Do It?"

"Well," I said, sitting down on the side of the bed where she'd indicated. "The truth is . . ."

Lucy's eyes widened. "Yes?"

"Basically . . ." I took a deep breath. "I jumped his bones."

Lucy squealed and squirmed in her seat. That's when I noticed that the magazine she'd been reading with such intense concentration had been an SAT prep book.

Wow. She really *did* love Harold.

"So what happened, EXACTLY?" she wanted to know. "You used the foam, right? And he used a condom? Because you have to use both. Heather Birnbaum just used condoms and got knocked up and had to go live with her aunt in Kentucky."

"We used the foam," I said. "And the condoms. Thank you for that."

"Did you—you know?" Lucy dropped her voice to a whisper.

"I think it's going to take some practice," I said, starting to blush, "for that to happen. But we'll get there."

"REALLY?" Lucy looked excited. "Tiffany always said it would work. Practicing with the handheld shower nozzle and all. But I didn't believe her. It's good to know she wasn't totally lying."

I looked at her curiously.

"Well," I said, "I mean, haven't you had some personal experience with it yourself? I mean, what about you and Jack?"

"JACK?" Lucy laughed as if this were hysterically funny. "Oh my God, JACK!"

I stared at her.

"But . . ." Something was not computing. "Lucy, you and Jack—you two Did It, right?"

Lucy made a face.

"Ew! Me? With JACK? Never!"

"Wait." I stared at her even harder. "So . . . you're . . . you're a VIRGIN?"

"Well, of course." Lucy looked puzzled. "What did you think?"

"But you and Jack went out for, like, three years!"

"So?" For someone who had so blithely (SAT word meaning "in a joyous manner") given me birth control and sex tips, Lucy looked extremely indignant at the suggestion that she herself might not be pure as the driven snow. "I mean, he *wanted* to, but I was like, No way, José!"

"But, Lucy," I cried. "The foam! And the condoms! You're the one who got them for me!"

"Well, of course," Lucy said matter-of-factly. "I couldn't let you go to the store and get them yourself and have it be all over the *National Enquirer*. I mean, that was before you made it so obvious that you don't care WHO knows your business by announcing it on national television. But that doesn't mean *I* ever used it. Foam, I mean. I just heard about it, you know. From Tiffany."

"But"—and this was the part that I was having the most trouble processing—"the other day, in the cafeteria. You called yourself a slut."

"So?" Lucy tossed some of her shimmery red-gold hair. "So did Catherine."

I stared at her, completely shocked. "So you . . . you just did that for me? And you and Jack—all that time—you never . . . you never . . ."

"Did It?" Lucy shook her head. "No way. I told you. He wasn't The One."

"But . . . but you thought he was. For a long time. You can't tell me you didn't. You even told me he was your first!"

"My first LOVE," Lucy said. "Not my first . . . you know."

"But . . ." I couldn't believe what I was hearing. "Why?"

"I don't know." Lucy shrugged. "I mean, yeah, I guess I thought sometimes he might be. The right guy. But I never knew. You know? Not the way you know about David. Or I know about Harold."

"You think *Harold* is The . . . One?" I asked.

I must have wrinkled my nose as I said it or something, though, because Lucy sounded defensive as she said, "Yes, I do. Why? What's wrong with Harold?"

"Nothing," I said quickly. "I'm sure you two will be very happy together. After, you know. You pass your SATs, and everything."

Apparently mollified, Lucy said, "So tell me all about it. Did it hurt the first time? Did his parents suspect? Where'd you guys Do It, his room or yours? What about the Secret Service? They weren't around, were they? What about—"

Her questions went on and on.

And even though I felt way too dazed to answer them, I totally tried. Because I fully owed her. Way more now than I'd ever even realized.

It was the least I could do to repay her.

Besides, what are sisters for?

"Sam! You showed!" Dauntra waved at me wildly from behind the cash register when I showed up for my shift later that day.

Well, so much for her being mad at me. I'd fully thought she would be. On account of my having turned out to have been a mouthpiece for the president's fascist initiative after all.

Although I *had* refused to go along with it at the last minute.

"Hey, D," I said, ducking beneath the counter to join her. "How was your Thanksgiving?"

"Bitchin'," Dauntra said. "I thought you were spending the weekend at your grandma's."

"I was," I said. "But I ended up going to Camp David, instead."

Dauntra hooted. "Camp *David*? Where the president spends his downtime?"

"That'd be the one," I said.

"Man." Dauntra shook her head. "And he LET you? After you dissed him like that on national TV?"

"I didn't dis him," I said uncomfortably. "I just pointed out to him that there might be a better way than, um, the one he was suggesting."

"Pointed out to him," Dauntra echoed with a grin. "Man, you are so cool."

I looked over my shoulder, wondering who she could be talking about. But the only other people in the store were some ninja geeks over by the Kurosawa shelves.

"Who?" I asked. "ME?"

"Yes, you," Dauntra said. "None of us can stop talking about how you totally put the Man in his place, and without even staging a die-in."

"Um," I said, not really sure what she was talking about, but pleased all the same. I mean, there aren't many people who actually think I'm cool. Except for my boyfriend, of course. And, it turns out, my big sister. "Thanks."

"I'm serious. Kevin wants to know if you want to come over some time. You know. To hang out."

"At your place?" My heart skipped a beat. I never imagined I'd ever get asked to "hang out" with someone as fabulous as Dauntra. I mean, we were work friends, and all that. But outside work? "Sure. I'd love to. Can I bring David?"

"The first kid?" Dauntra shrugged. "Why not? It'll be a hoot. Oh, and hey, you inspired me." She reached inside her backpack, pulled out a neatly folded piece of paper, and handed it to me. "When Stan comes over to check my bag tonight, I'm giving him this."

"What is it?" I asked, unfolding it.

"An e-mail," Dauntra said proudly. "From my lawyer. At the ACLU. She's taking on my case. I decided it might work better than maple syrup. You know. To go the Samantha Madison route."

I blinked at her. "Hiring a lawyer from the

ACLU to keep your employer from going through your backpack for stolen goods at the end of your shift is going the Samantha Madison route?"

"Totally," Dauntra said. "Way better than a die-in. You certainly don't get your clothes as dirty. And by the time my new lawyer's done with the management here, I bet I'll own this place."

"Wow," I said, handing the e-mail back to her. "I'm impressed."

"Well, you should be. It's all 'cause of you. Hey, did you have a good time?"

I glanced at her curiously. "A good time?"

"At Camp David. What'd you guys do there, anyway? It must have been pretty boring. It was raining the whole time, right?"

"Oh," I said, fiddling with the *Love Means . . . Willing to Wait* pin in the Sally action figure's chest. "We found stuff to do."

"Oh my God."

Something in Dauntra's voice made me look up. She was staring down at me quite intently.

"Oh my God, Sam," she said. "Did you and David . . . *DO* IT?"

"Um." I felt my cheeks—as they had a million

times already that day—start to heat up. I looked around to see if Chuck or Stan or anyone else was nearby.

But the only person in the store besides us was Mr. Wade, who was busy poring over some new arrivals in the Arts section.

"Um," I said. There was no reason to feel defensive. This wasn't Kris Parks. This was *Dauntra*. Dauntra wasn't going to call me a slut. Dauntra would never call anyone a slut. Except maybe Britney Spears. But that was only natural.

"Yeah," I said, even though my mouth suddenly felt very dry. "We did."

And Dauntra, leaning an elbow against the cash register, propped her chin in her hand, sighed, and asked me dreamily, "Wasn't it FUN?"

I blinked. "Wasn't what fun?"

"Excuse me." Mr. Wade had wandered up to the counter. "I was wondering if you have a DVD ordered in yet. The name is Wade, W—"

"A–D–E," Dauntra said tiredly. "Dude, we KNOW your name. You're in here every day, for crying out loud!"

Mr. Wade looked taken aback. "Oh," he said. "I didn't think you'd remember me."

"Dude," Dauntra said, reaching for the DVD

he'd ordered. "Get real. You're unforgettable." Then, looking back at me, she said, "Sex. I meant, wasn't sex fun?"

I glanced at Mr. Wade, whose eyes were goggling out from underneath his beret. Then I looked back at Dauntra with a grin.

"Yes," I said. "Yes, it really was."

"How was your Thanksgiving weekend?"

That's what David asked me the next time we saw each other, which wasn't until Susan Boone's life drawing class the following Tuesday.

He was grinning wolfishly, a clear sign he was joking. But I answered him with all sincerity just the same:

"You know what?" I said. "It was pretty good. How was yours?"

"Awesome." He winked. "Best Thanksgiving ever."

We both sat there grinning idiotically at each other until Rob came bustling by with his drawing pad, muttering over the fact that he'd forgotten his soft lead pencils. Then, remembering we weren't exactly alone, David and I both busied ourselves setting up our charcoal and erasers.

But I for one was still smiling. Because all that

stuff I'd been worried about—you know, about how after couples have sex, that's all they ever think about or do?

It isn't true. I mean, I *think* about it. A lot.

But it's not *all* I think about.

And I know it's not all David thinks about, either. I can tell, because essentially, our relationship hasn't really changed. He still calls me last thing every night, and first thing every morning, like always.

Which was how he was one of the first people I told that my house wasn't the only place that had undergone some Big Changes. When I got to school on Monday, I'd found a few changes had been made there, too, while we'd all been away on Thanksgiving break . . . the biggest one being that Right Way had disbanded, due to all of its members—save one, namely Kris Parks—dropping out.

But that wasn't all. I'd also found out that Kris Parks? Yeah, she was no longer president of the junior class. Because you can't break a school conduct code (as Kris had, in calling me a slut in front of so many witnesses) and maintain your student government position, because, as a student government representative, you're supposed to be an example to the rest of the student population.

So, Frau Rider, our eleventh grade advisor, had to appoint the vice president as chief class officer until new elections could be held in the spring.

A bunch of people—well, okay, mainly Catherine, Deb Mullins, Lucy, and Harold— thought *I* should run. For class president.

But I really have quite enough to do, thank you, what with art lessons, my job, and teen ambassador stuff.

Besides, to be president of your class at school, you actually have to CARE about your school. And I so don't. Care about my school, I mean.

But I have to admit, I'm starting to like it a little better these days.

"Hey, guess who's going to California this coming weekend for a fund-raiser?" David asked me.

"Let me guess," I said, picking up my drawing pad and turning to a nice, clean page. "Your parents."

"Yeah. And they'll be gone till Sunday night. I'll have that big, white house all to myself."

"How nice for you," I said. "You can dance

around in your underwear and sunglasses to some Bob Seger."

"I was thinking it'd be more fun if you came over," David said. "We got the new Mel Gibson movie. You know, the one that just came out."

"I'll have to check with my parents," I said. "But . . . I imagine they'll say yes."

"Excellent," David said, doing his best Mr. Burns.

"Hello, everyone." Susan Boone came rushing in, followed, much more slowly, by the lethargic (SAT word meaning "morbidly drowsy") Terry. "Are we all here? Is everyone ready? Terry, if you wouldn't mind . . ."

Terry took off his robe and laid down on the raised platform. It wasn't long before he fell asleep, his chest rising and falling with gentle snores.

And this time, when I drew him, I tried to concentrate on the whole, and not the parts. I roughed in the room around him, and then his place in it, trying to build my drawing the way you build a house . . . from the frame up, keeping in mind that there had to be a balance between the subject of my drawing and the background supporting it. . . .

And I guess I succeeded, because when it came time for the critique of our evening's work, Susan was pleased with my results.

"Very good, Sam," she said, about my drawing. "You're really learning."

"Yes," I said, with some surprise. "I guess I really am."

For all the books about Sam and more by

MEG CABOT

check out the following pages!

You'll find:

- An excerpt from *All-American Girl*, the first book featuring Samantha Madison

- Blurbs about Meg's other exciting books

- Info on the Princess Diaries series

Still not enough?

For even more about Meg Cabot, go to:

www.harperteen.com/megcabot

Samantha Madison saves the day!
(sort of)
in Meg Cabot's

ALL-AMERICAN GIRL

IT ONLY took about two hours for it
to get all the way around John Adams Preparatory
School that I was bringing the president's son with me
as my date to Kris Parks's party on Saturday night.

For some reason this was more interesting to
people than the fact that I had stopped a bullet from
entering the skull of our nation's leader, or that I was
the country's new teen ambassador to the UN.
While I could not help but be thankful that I was no
longer constantly being complimented on my bravery—all the more upsetting because I truly did not
believe what I had done had been all that brave—it
was somewhat disconcerting that everyone was,
instead, making jokes about what might or might
not have gone on between the president's son and
me in the Lincoln Bedroom.

"Look, you're taking this the wrong way," Lucy

said when I remarked upon this at the kitchen table after school. "The fact that you and this David dude are an item—DO NOT PINCH ME AGAIN—is only going to elevate your already sky-high stock. You, Sam, are the new It Girl of Adams Prep. If you would just give up the whole black-on-black thing, you could be voted prom queen like *that*." Lucy snapped her fingers in the air.

"Well, I don't want to be prom queen," I said. "I just want things to be back to normal."

"I'm going to take a wild guess that *that*'s not going to happen real soon," Jack said. He pointed to the reporters we could see holding their cameras up over the backyard fence, hoping to snap a picture of us through the glass atrium.

"Jesu Cristo," Theresa said, and she went to the phone to call the police again.

I sunk my chin down into my hand and went, "I just don't see why you had to tell everybody that. I mean, it is so far from the truth." I said this very clearly, so that Jack would hear. I mean, I wanted to make sure he knew that, if ever he changed his mind about Lucy, I was still available.

"How was I supposed to know what the truth is?" Lucy asked primly. "You won't tell me where the two of you disappeared to last night."

4

I couldn't believe she would even bring any of that up in front of Jack. Although seeing as how Lucy was unaware of Jack's status as my soul mate, I guess I couldn't really blame her.

"Because it isn't any of your business!" I cried. "I mean, you don't tell me every single thing you and Jack do together."

"Ha!" Lucy stabbed a finger at me, her smile triumphant. "I *knew* it! You two *are* going out!"

"No, we aren't," I said. "I didn't say that."

"Yes, you did. You just admitted it. You said, 'You don't tell me every single thing you and Jack do together,' which must mean you and David are going out just like Jack and I are."

"No," I said. "It doesn't mean that at all—"

My extremely lucid argument was interrupted, however, by Theresa, who, having gotten off the phone with the police, had then gone to intercept a package that had arrived by special delivery.

"For you," she said, setting the package down in front of me. "From the White House, the man said."

We all looked down at the package.

"See," Lucy said. "It's from David. I told you that you two are going out."

"It isn't from David," I said, opening it. "And we aren't going out."

Katie Ellison doesn't mean to be a liar, liar

Pants on fire

Katie Ellison has everything going for her senior year—a great job, two boyfriends, and a good shot at being crowned Quahog Princess of her small coastal town in Connecticut. So why does Tommy Sullivan have to come back into her life? Sure, they used to be friends, but that was before the huge screwup that turned their whole town against him. Now he's back, and making Katie's perfect life a total disaster. Can the Quahog Princess and the *freak* have anything in common? Could they even be falling for each other?

Is it just bad luck . . . or could it be witchcraft?

Is she just the unluckiest girl on the planet, or could Jean "Jinx" Honeychurch be . . . a witch?

Since the day she was born, Jinx has been a lightning rod for bad luck—everything just seems to go wrong when she's around. But she's sure her luck is going to change, now that she's moving to New York City to stay with her aunt, uncle, and super-sweet cousin Tory. Because things can only get better, right? Wrong! Not only is Tory not super-sweet anymore, she thinks she's a witch. She even has a coven of other pretty Upper East Side girls. Jinx is afraid they might hurt someone with their "magic," but she isn't sure how to stop them. Could Jinx's bad luck be the thing that saves the day?

*Girl-next-door Jenny Greenley goes stir-crazy
(or star-crazy?) in Meg Cabot's*

TEEN IDOL

Jenny Greenley's good at solving problems—so good she's the school paper's anonymous advice columnist. But when nineteen-year-old screen sensation Luke Striker comes to Jenny's small town to research a role, he creates havoc that even level-headed Jenny isn't sure she can repair . . . especially since she's right in the middle of all of it. Can Jenny, who always manages to be there for everybody else, learn to take her own advice, and find true love at last?

Does Steph have what it takes?

HOW TO BE *Popular*

Everyone wants to be popular—or at least, Stephanie Landry does. Steph's been the least popular girl in her class since a certain cherry Super Big Gulp catastrophe five years earlier. And she's determined to get in with the It Crowd this year—no matter what! After all, Steph's got a secret weapon: an old book called—what else?—*How to Be Popular*.

Turns out . . . it's easy to become popular. What isn't so easy? Staying that way!

Ellie has a hunch that nothing is as it seems in

 # AVALON HIGH

Avalon High seems like a typical school, with typical students. There's Lance, the jock. Jennifer, the cheerleader. And Will, senior class president, quarterback, and all-around good guy. But not everyone at Avalon High is who they appear to be . . . not even, as new student Ellie is about to discover, herself. What part does she play in the drama that is unfolding? What if the chain of coincidences she has pieced together means—like the court of King Arthur—tragedy is fast approaching Avalon High? Worst of all, what if there's nothing she can do about it?

Ellie's story continues in the manga series

Don't miss the thrilling sequels to *Avalon High*:

the mediator

Suze can see ghosts. Which is kind of a pain most of the time, but when Suze moves to California and finds Jesse, the ghost of a nineteenth-century hottie haunting her bedroom, things begin to look up.

Shadowland

Ninth Key

Reunion

Darkest Hour

Haunted

Twilight

1-800-WHERE-R-YOU

Ever since a freakish lightning strike, Jessica Mastriani has had the psychic ability to locate missing people. But her life is anything but easy. If you had the gift, would you use it?

WHEN LIGHTNING STRIKES

CODE NAME CASSANDRA

SAFE HOUSE

SANCTUARY

MISSING YOU

Meg Cabot is also the author of the Princess Diaries series, upon which the Disney movies are based. In the books, though, Princess Mia has yield-sign-shaped hair, lives in New York, and Fat Louie is orange. And those are the least of the differences. The following is a complete list of the Princess Diaries books:

The Princess Diaries

THE PRINCESS DIARIES, VOLUME II:
Princess in the Spotlight

THE PRINCESS DIARIES, VOLUME III:
Princess in Love

THE PRINCESS DIARIES, VOLUME IV:
Princess in Waiting

Valentine Princess:
A PRINCESS DIARIES BOOK (VOLUME IV AND A QUARTER)

THE PRINCESS DIARIES, VOLUME IV AND A HALF:
Project Princess

THE PRINCESS DIARIES, VOLUME V:
Princess in Pink

But wait!
There's more by Meg:

NICOLA AND THE VISCOUNT

VICTORIA AND THE ROGUE